ERNEST DOWSON
COLLECTED SHORTER FICTION

A Case of Conscience

I.

It was in Brittany, and the apples were already acquiring
a sudden autumnal tint amid their greens and yellows,
though autumn was not yet; and the country lay very still
and fair, in the sunset which had befallen softly and
suddenly as is the fashion there. A man and a girl
stood, looking down in silence at the village Ploumariel,
from their post of vantage half way up the hill: at
its lichened church spire, dotted with little gables
like dove-cotes; at the slated roof of its market; at its
quiet white houses. The man's eyes rested on it
complacently, with the enjoyment of the artist: finding
it charming; the girl's a little absently, as one who
had seen it very often before. She was pretty and
very young; but her gray, serious eyes, the poise
of her head, with its rebellious brown hair braided
plainly gave her a little air of dignity, of reserve which
sat piquantly upon her youth. In one ungloved hand,
that was brown from the sun but very beautiful, she
held an old parasol; the other played absently with
a bit of purple heather. Presently she began to
speak, using English, just coloured by a foreign
accent that made her speech prettier.
'You make me afraid;' she said, turning her large,
troubled eyes on her companion, 'you make me afraid,—
of myself, chiefly: but a little, of you. You suggest
so much to me that is new, strange, terrible: when
you speak, I am troubled: all my old landmarks
appear to vanish; I even hardly know right from wrong.

---

*Page 1 of Dowson's signed autograph ms of 'A Case of Conscience'; MA 1905 in
The Pierpont Morgan Library, New York (reduced). Photography: Joseph Zehavi.*

TO
HILARY
AND
TO
NEIL

Ernest Dowson
Collected Shorter Fiction

Edited by

Monica Borg

and

R. K. R. Thornton

Birmingham University Press
2003

First published in the United Kingdom by:

The University of Birmingham Press,
University of Birmingham,
Edgbaston, Birmingham, B15 2TT, UK.

ISBN 1-902459-25-3

British Library Cataloguing in Publication data
A CIP catalogue record for this book is available from the British Library.

Printed in Great Britain by Central Printing Services, University of Birmingham.

CONTENTS

ACKNOWLEDGEMENTS

We would like to thank the staff of the various libraries where we have consulted editions of Dowson: the British Library, the Library of the University of Birmingham, the Newcastle upon Tyne Literary and Philosophical Society, and Newcastle upon Tyne City Library. We would like to acknowledge the permission of the Pierpont Morgan Library to reproduce material from their manuscript MA 1905, the manuscript of 'A Case of Conscience', and to thank the staff there who were so helpful in answering our queries, particularly Inge Dupont and Christine Nelson.

INTRODUCTION

Ernest Dowson is best known as a poet; but he devoted a great deal of his time to prose, giving close attention to his various projects for novels, stories and translations, which were substantially his bread and butter. For his longer fiction he usually worked in collaboration with his friend Arthur Moore (1866-1952), with whom he wrote *A Comedy of Masks* (1893) and *Adrian Rome* (1899), their two published novels. Their mode of collaboration was to write the chapters turn and turn about in notebooks which they passed from one to the other. Before the success of those two novels, the pair had written *The Passion of Dr Ludovicus*, which was begun at Oxford and went to several publishers in 1889, but was accepted by none. They began *Felix Martyr* in 1889, but that too never found a publisher and was perhaps not ever completed. Dowson's apprenticeship also included the writing of a 'shocker' (again offered to publishers but not accepted) and a novel called *Madame de Viole* in the late 1880s. None of this apprentice work was published. Dowson made a number of translations, usually from the French, including Zola's *La Terre* (1894), Couperus's *Majesty* (1894), Balzac's *La Fille aux yeux d'or* (1896), and Choderlos de Laclos' *Liaisons Dangeureuses* (1898), though he also helped G. A. Greene and Arthur Cecil Hillier in translating Richard Muther's *The History of Modern Painting* (1895-6) from the German.

Throughout his central creative period in the first half of the nineties Dowson also produced short stories, and the nine pieces which we print are all that he wrote. In saying this, we are excluding the brief prose poems, which will appear in the poetic companion to this volume and belong more firmly to the tradition of heightened poetic prose than with his fiction, written in discipleship to Henry James and the French masters.

His first published story appeared in January 1888 in *Temple Bar* (described on its title page as 'A London Magazine For Town and Country Readers'), followed by two stories in *Macmillan's Magazine* in February 1890 and August 1891 (alongside writers like Augustine Birrell, W. H. Hudson, Aubrey de Vere and Bret Harte); but Dowson soon seemed to prefer the sympathetic environment of *The Century Guild Hobby Horse* (and its later reincarnation, *The Hobby Horse*), *The Yellow Book* and *The Savoy*.

In 1893 he submitted proposals for a volume to contain his first four stories (all so far published). The proposal was read, apparently for a second time, by his fellow Rhymer Richard Le Gallienne, who wrote the following report for the publisher Elkin Mathews:

> Mr. Dowson applies very delicate literary treatment to somewhat hackneyed themes – at least in the case of two of his stories, 'The Souvenirs of an Egoist' and 'The Story of a Violin'. The great musical composer who started life as an organ-grinder, the second violin in an orchestra, poor and unknown, who was once the guardian and tutor of the fashionable prima donna (like little Bows in 'Pendennis') are very old acquaintances in fiction. In Messrs. Dowson and Moore's 'Comedy of Masks' one was struck with the concentration of theme and freshness of treatment. However, if these well-known types have been done before, they have seldom been done better. Of the other two, 'A Case of Conscience' is very much in the manner of Mr. Wedmore's 'Pastorals', – 'A Last Love at Pornic' for example – delicate, vague, and generally 'nice', but amounting to little. 'The Diary of a Successful Man' is probably the most original – but the title should certainly be changed. It is a rough and ready label, with no true relation to the story. 'The Story of a Violin' is also an unfortunate title, as nothing is more hackneyed than the conventional Stradivarius story the title will inevitably suggest. 'Souvenirs of an Egoist' is a taking title, and so, I suppose, had better be left, but it suggests far more than the story fulfils.

On the whole, having regard to the delicacy of the treatment, *and the success of 'A Comedy of Masks'* (which was not a consideration when I first read these stories) I would advise you to accept these as an instalment of a volume, (they are not big enough to make one themselves) with the promise that the stories to come should be more striking, more original in theme – not less so, not mere makeweights – than those under consideration.

(quoted in *Letters*, 263-4)[1].

Mathews contacted Dowson, presumably on the strength of this report, and Dowson replied to Elkin Mathews and John Lane (who still at that time worked jointly under the sign of the Bodley Head) on c.30 November 1893:

I am obliged to you for your letter with reference to my stories. Would you kindly let me know, about how much more material you would require to make up a volume uniform with 'Keynotes'? There is a story of mine, recently published in the 'Hobby Horse', which I could include, if it should meet with your approval – and I have one story nearly completed, and another, unpublished, which I could send you shortly.

If this would not be sufficient, I am afraid I should not be able to add anything more until the summer, for I am at present engaged upon a translation [of Zola's *La Terre*], which occupies, & will occupy, all my time until the beginning of May (*Letters*, 301).

As things turned out, although a volume of Dowson's stories was advertised as appearing 'shortly' in Mathews's advertisement in *The Hobby Horse* number 3 of 1894, the book was not published until 1895, by Mathews alone; and the only additional story was the one from *The Hobby Horse* which Dowson had mentioned: 'The Statute of Limitations'. Perhaps Dowson took a little notice of Le Gallienne's advice in placing first the story Le Gallienne had called 'the most original' and reverting to his earlier title for 'An Orchestral Violin'. A letter to Elkin Mathews, which Dowson confusingly signed with a mis-spelling of Mathews's own name, suggests that he was in a troubled state: 'The order of the stories will do very well as they are. It would certainly be not worth while changing them now' (*Letters*, 309). He shows more interest in the size of the type used for the dedication, which offers the book as a tribute – as was so much of what Dowson did – 'To Missie (A. F.)'. For the rest of his life Dowson carried with him a copy of *Dilemmas* and wrote the places and dates of his travels on this dedication page (see illustration in *Letters*, facing page 392). *Dilemmas* (1895) itself, reviewed in *The Realm* in June, was a disappointingly poorly produced edition. Dowson's other stories were never collected in his lifetime.

The order in which we print the stories is a simple decision, but needs comment. One could arrange them in the order in which they were written and published, which would be as follows:

'Souvenirs of an Egoist', January 1888
'The Diary of a Successful Man', February 1890
'An Orchestral Violin', August 1891
'A Case of Conscience', January 1891
'The Statute of Limitations', January 1893
'Apple Blossom in Brittany', October 1894
'The Eyes of Pride', January 1896
'Countess Marie of the Angels', April 1896
'The Dying of Francis Donne', August 1896

But Dowson may have had some principle in mind in his arrangement of the first five stories when he published them in *Dilemmas*, if only to lead with his best work. It was his first book and, in spite of his distracted air, he can be expected to have given the matter some thought. So we have followed his arrangement there, which is: 'The Diary of a Successful Man', 'A Case of Conscience', 'An Orchestral Violin', 'Souvenirs of and Egoist' and 'The Statute of Limitations' and from then on we follow the chronological order in which the stories were published.

This edition of Dowson's nine short stories, the first since Mark Longaker's 1947 edition, seeks to rescue Dowson's short fiction from the neglect it has suffered for more than half a century; and this introduction endeavours to bring into focus the link that Dowson's fictional project established with the radical and disruptive agenda of the *fin-de-siècle* Decadence, and argues for the central role that his stories play in delineating his Decadent identity.

Dowson's Fictional Project

A close look at Ernest Dowson's short stories shows that the writer's prose can be more genuinely Decadent than his poetry, especially if by Decadence we refer to that turbulent cultural crisis that hit *fin-de-siècle* Britain and the feelings of dissatisfaction, unrest and rebelliousness it generated amongst the artists and writers of the avant-garde. In their spectacular disintegration of form and content, the nine stories that Dowson contributed to various 'little' journals and magazines of the nineties not only represent a subversive response to this crisis but also exemplify that 'anarchic' strand of the literary Decadence as presented in the theories of Paul Bourget and Friedrich Nietzsche.

However, despite the obvious affinity that Dowson's prose has with this anarchic aspect of the Decadence, it was not his prose which ultimately earned him his Decadent reputation. A brief overview of the critical appraisals of Dowson's literary works shows that it was his verse which played the major role in establishing his identity as an exponent of the British Decadence, and it was his poetry, not his prose, which continued to capture the critical imagination, both in his times and throughout the twentieth century. Dowson himself had in his lifetime expressed concern about the obvious bias with which contemporary critics continued to treat his poetry when he told Frank Harris that he much preferred his prose to his verse.[2] Arthur Symons, who met him often in the 1890s, wrote in his introduction to *The Poems of Ernest Dowson* (1902) that 'Dowson was the only poet I ever knew who cared more for his prose than his verse'. He often wrote deprecatingly of his verse and dismissed his poetry as experiments or as 'verses making for mere sound, & music, with just a suggestion of sense, or hardly that; a vague Verlainesque emotion. They are not successful enough to send you' (to Arthur Moore, 20 March 1891, *Letters*, 190).

Yet, despite Dowson's efforts to focus attention on his prose, it was poetry which continued to fascinate 1890s scholars. So powerful was the influence of Dowson's poetic production on the critical imagination, that whenever the short stories were taken into consideration they were seen through the romantic aesthetic lens which tinted the writer's poetic vision. Thus, in 1947, in the last edition of Dowson's stories, Mark Longaker set down Dowson's prose tales as 'chaste, restrained records' of that suffering and devotion to an ideal, which are registered in the writer's poetry;[3] while in 1974 Keith Cushman read Dowson's stories as 'pale, delicate variations' on his characteristic poetic themes of 'lost love and the tragic gap between the flux of life and the perfection of art.'[4] In 1992, Chris Snodgrass provided fresh insight on the writer's work when he argued that Schopenhauer's philosophy furnished a 'synthesizing locus' for Dowson's vision. Yet, he, too, went on to interpret some of the Decadent's most original fictional representations as mere reiterations of his poetic motifs.[5] In his recent biography, *Madder Music, Stronger Wine*, Jad Adams testifies to the unrelenting appeal that Dowson's poetry continues to exercise on scholars to this day. Activating the familiar rhetoric of the superiority of Dowson's poetic production, Adams remarks that the writer's verse 'is incomparably better than his prose and the prose would be all but forgotten were it not for his fame as a poet.'[6] Adams has a point here; yet, like most scholars who have so far written on Dowson, he fails to address the issue of the writer's aesthetic and cultural radicalism or examine the writer's work in relation to that crisis of values, self and representation which, as an exponent of the Decadence, Dowson simultaneously expressed and sought to precipitate.

A spectacle of disintegration

Several critics have expressed dissatisfaction with Dowson's short stories, criticizing them for their lack of compelling plot and vivid characterization.[7] Such remarks, prompted undoubtedly by the desire to find that 'breeding and restraint'[8] which scholars invariably encountered in Dowson the poet and automatically expected to find in Dowson the short-story writer, are misleading, for it is precisely Dowson's lack of restraint, the fragmentary nature of his plots and his split, diffuse and ambiguous characters which best express his Decadence, his radicalism and his modernity. As Dowson himself suggested in a note he wrote in praise of Olive Schreiner's controversial *The Story of an African Farm*, his fictional project was not meant to reinforce established narrative traditions or support the conservative politics embraced by such contemporaries as Rider Haggard, who was engaged in reviving the male adventure tale.[9] 'The time for romance, for novels written in the stage method, is gone', Dowson wrote. 'In a worldly decaying civilization, in an age of nostalgia like the present – what is the meaning of Mr. Rider Haggard? He is an anachronism' (*Letters*, 10). He therefore set out to accomplish a project which was consciously innovative and subversive, producing a number of short stories which, in their spectacular vandalisation of form and content, established a connection with the 'anarchic' agenda of the literary and artistic Decadence. In Dowson's short stories, linguistic and genre boundaries are duly transgressed and the neat and ordered categories of traditional narrative are systematically ransacked. This disintegrating scenario acts as the background for a number of effete Decadents and rebellious New Women, notoriously subversive *fin-de-siècle* figures, through whom Dowson expresses his dissent on current sexual and gender roles, his sympathy with the women's struggle for emancipation and his outrage against the strictures placed on individual freedom by social duty and morality.

Victor Plarr, Dowson's contemporary, was one of the first critics to draw attention to Dowson's love of linguistic anarchy when he noted that his style was punctuated by 'petulant Gallicisms'.[10] In most of the writer's stories, the smooth flowing order of the English idiom is disrupted by words, expressions and sometimes whole paragraphs[11] from French or Latin. Not only are the linguistic frontiers systematically transgressed, but conventional genre boundaries are also blurred when disparate narrating frames are collapsed within the context of the same story. In 'The Diary of a Successful Man', the diaristic mode of narration rubs uneasy shoulders with the epistolary form, prose subsides impetuously into verse and the mundane tone of ordinary language drops abruptly to modulate into the sacred idiom of religion, chant and prayer. The chaotic, pastiche-like quality of this story is at its most spectacular when Dion, the protagonist/narrator, unrealistically transcribes his beloved's letter (9) as well as a few strophes and antistrophes of the litany in his diary (14). Similarly, in 'The Statute of Limitations', prose is violated by verse when a whole stanza from Christina Rossetti's 'The Prince's Progress' is recorded in the narrative (80).

Recurrent flashbacks, fade-outs as well as open-ended and unresolved plot structures also stage a show of chaos and anarchy, frustrating that drift towards order and closure which featured in more conventional fictional forms. At the end of 'The Statute of Limitations', the reader is abandoned to doubt and is left to decide for him/herself whether Garth, the protagonist, has committed suicide or whether he has simply had an accident on board the ship that was taking him home to his intended. Similarly, 'An Orchestral Violin' ends with an unanswered question, the unresolved plot structure aligning itself with the masculinity crisis of the Decadent narrator, whose failure to establish control over his plot signifies a broader loss of male power over discourse and representation.

The Chinese-box structure of 'Souvenirs of an Egoist' also displays that formal disjointedness through which Dowson's stories at once pay homage to the anarchic aesthetics of the Decadence and engage with the techniques of Modernism. The narrative thread of this story leaps spasmodically backwards and forwards in time as the narrator projects, through flashback upon flashback, a self image designed to illustrate the amoral and supreme egoism of the *fin-de-siècle* Decadent, whose titanic subjectivity leads him to seek blind but supreme gratification in artistic expression. In its deployment of typically Freudian sexual configurations, this short story also anticipates the discourses of psychoanalysis. Anton's success in the world of music is seen as being premised on the conviction of his masculine superiority, a phallic sense of plenitude and self-sufficiency acquired in his early formative years *vis-à-vis* the self-effacing, 'empty' femininity of Ninette. But what is more intriguing about this tale is that, while it engages with the subversive aesthetics of the Decadence and the discourses of psychoanalysis, it seems to stumble, as if by chance, into narrating techniques we would now recognise as Postmodernist. Anton, the protagonist narrator, occasionally digresses into stretches of metafictional commentary, providing the reader with glimpses of the 'over-intrusive visibly inventing narrator', a ploy which Patricia Waugh has listed as a typical feature of Postmodernist aesthetics.[12] In one of the flashbacks designed to highlight the events which led to the acquisition of the violin, a cardinal event in the story, Anton suddenly snaps the narrative thread and plunges deliberately into a critique designed to undermine the purposive, didactic aesthetics of traditional fiction. Addressing himself directly to the reader, Anton alerts her/him to the way in which seemingly innocent events, such as the one he was illustrating in his story, would be exploited to impart a lesson in bourgeois morals and ethics. Ninette, the little orphan girl Anton has befriended in the back-streets of Paris, has been presented with the exorbitant sum of a gold *louis* for a nosegay she has sold to a gentleman outside the *Opéra* in Paris. The narrator remarks:

> I believe the good little boy and girl in the story-books would have immediately sought out the unfortunate gentleman and bid him rectify his mistake, generally receiving, so the legend runs, a far larger bonus as a reward of their integrity (60).

Anton, posing as a subversive Decadent narrator, chooses to eschew melodrama, idealism and morality for a more realistic outcome and so, he specifies, Ninette decides to pocket the money and to purchase the violin that her little friend, Anton, had long desired. The narrator here intervenes not only to discourage the reader, in a postmodernist fashion, from mistaking fictional representation for reality but also to show that as a Decadent he chooses to make Art triumph over all considerations of ethics and morality.

The amoralistic streak of this story is reinforced towards the end of the narrative. Having decided to reward the organ player for the pleasant memories she has evoked by sending her a coin, Anton deliberately refrains from ensuring that his manservant does not pocket the money himself. At this point, Anton again swerves away from his plot in a Postmodernist fashion, to deliver a critique of that idealism and sentimentality which pervaded Victorian romance fiction:

> Now if I was writing a romance, what a chance I have got. I should tell you how my organ-grinder turned out to be no other than Ninette. . . . Then what scope for a pathetic scene of reconciliation and forgiveness – the whole to conclude with a peal of marriage bells, two people living together 'happy ever after.' But I am not writing a romance (70).

There is little doubt that Anton, posing as narrator, is here acting as the mouthpiece for the Decadence which Dowson embraced. Through a tale which allegedly sets out to illustrate the supreme egoism of the *fin-de-siècle* Decadent, Dowson weaves a critical subtext designed to lash out at the didacticism, sentimentalism and idealism which played a central role in current literary and artistic conventions.

Incoherent Subjects, Decadent Men and New Women

Not only do Dowson's stories stage a drama of formal and stylistic disintegration but they also adhere to strategies of character representation which perform, *vis-à-vis* the manly and womanly ideals extolled by bourgeois culture, radical ideological work. Far from featuring characters in the 'full career of action',[13] Dowson's fiction is replete with sympathetic representations of individuals whose action exhausts itself exclusively on the thinking plane. Dowson's protagonists are therefore not social agents but thinking or spiritual subjects;[14] they are often burdened with elusive and unknowable selves and, in the chaos, doubt and conflict that their split personalities generate, challenge current understandings which posit the subject primarily as an individual in control, a subject who possessed a coherent self that can be known and the knowledge that can capture it.

The protagonist/narrators in 'Souvenirs of an Egoist' and 'The Diary of a Successful Man' are confused, unstable and out of control. Both are perplexed by the dealings of a deceptive and highly ephemeral subconscious and both are portrayed as subjects who engage exclusively in prolonged and morbid self-reflection and self-analysis. Dowson's protagonists do not aspire to the active manly ideals of bourgeois culture for they are eternally paralyzed by doubt and conflict. Anton, in 'Souvenirs of an Egoist', may well have determined to embrace the philosophy of the Decadence and place Art above morality, artistic rigour above emotional fulfilment, but he achieves this at the cost of an agonizing psychic split. His steadfast determination to serve Art is repeatedly undermined by oppositional drives which propel him, despite his will, towards emotional fulfilment. Artistic expression, he learns, is intellectually gratifying but leaves an emotional void; emotional gratification is satisfying but is intellectually frustrating. 'I was very fond of Ninette' says Anton of the little girl who showered him with love and affection, but then admits that despite her warmth and generosity her company often made him feel 'fretful and discontented' (59). So in the end he decides to abandon her for the cold and unresponsive Lady Greville, who exemplifies artistic and intellectual gratification. But Anton's repressed emotional needs keep surfacing in his narrative in the form of recurring images of Ninette.

> But it is of Ninette, not Lady Greville, that I think to-night, Ninette's childish face that the dreary grinding organ brings up before me, not Lady Greville's aquiline nose and delicate artificial complexion (54).

In 'Souvenirs of an Egoist', Lady Greville and her nephew Felix who, like Anton, have embraced the religion of Art, also suffer from split personalities. Their pose as cynical Decadents, a requisite in the artistic circles they frequent, clashes violently with the more genuine and spontaneous demands of their romantic souls. Lady Greville, we are told, jealously guards a bundle of love letters in a secret drawer in her boudoir; while Felix, 'the prince of railers' (62), still suffers, despite his outward cynicism, from a past romantic attachment to a Parisian *grisette*.

While investigating the crises and dilemmas which afflicted the Decadent sensibility, Dowson conveys images of that impending neurosis which was to pervade the modern consciousness. Anton's vagrant life, which leads him eventually to the Parisian capital, his dual Anglo-Italian lineage, the violent dislocation from the margins of society into the heart of artistic prestige and affluence in the city, all index that social and geographic mobility which characterize the modern condition.

The sustained focus on the spiritual problems of the Decadent also led Dowson to stumble into the notion of the subconscious, anticipating, in his short stories, the twentieth century discourses of psychoanalysis. Dion, the narrator/protagonist of 'The Diary of a Successful Man' suffers, like the protagonists of 'Souvenirs of an Egoist', from a split self. However, the psychic rupture in this short story is more specifically formulated in terms of a conflict between conscious and subconscious drives. In the opening pages of his diary, Dion is able to project a positive image of himself as a man who has reached the heights of domestic bliss and professional success. But he soon discovers that this self-image has been fostered by a deceptive consciousness, which for years has sustained him with a false illusion of happiness. Dion, we learn, has suppressed in his subconscious an unhappiness which has afflicted him since he was rejected by Delphine, the love of his youth. This repressed emotion, however, eventually manages to overcome subterfuge and, propelling itself to the surface of the conscious mind, shatters Dion's illusion of happiness for ever:

> for once and for the last time, let me set myself down as a dreary fraud. I never forgot her, not for one hour or day, not even when it seemed to me that I had forgotten her most, not even when I married (15).

Learning that Delphine has joined the cloistered order of the Dames Rouges, and that therefore he will never be able to set eyes on her again, Dion is forced to acknowledge defeat:

> it seemed to me to-day, strangely enough, as though a certain candle of hope, of promise, of pleasant possibilities, which had flickered with more or less light for so many years, had suddenly gone out and left me alone in utter darkness (16).

By focusing exclusively on his male characters' split selves and by emphasising the dilemmas generated by their conflicting conscious and subconscious drives, Dowson conveys a prevalently spiritual image of male subjectivity. The only action these two characters engage in is self reflection, a morbid self-analysis which leads them to a heightened sense of pessimism and lands them in total social and intellectual paralysis. This mode of representing and understanding the male subject clashed violently with the bourgeois ideal of masculinity, a subject perceived as a social, not a solitary, being whose coherence and resourcefulness guaranteed his success in the public world of politics, commerce and industry. By deploying sympathetic images of split, incoherent and unstable male subjects, Decadents who dedicate themselves to non-purposive artistic activities and labyrinthine thought processes, Dowson's stories subversively disseminate imagery of what Herbert Marcuse was later to call the spiritual subject – a mode of perceiving subjectivity which clashed with an economy which relied upon resourceful and dynamic men for the realization of its capitalist, technological and imperialist projects.[15]

But if the split protagonist/narrators in 'Souvenirs of an Egoist' and 'The Diary of a Successful Man' question assumptions about the dynamism and coherence of the male subject, the resolute and rebellious female protagonists who feature in some of Dowson's short stories perform equally subversive ideological work. The strong-willed and talented Leonora Romanoff in 'An Orchestral Violin', Rosalind Lingard in 'The Eyes of Pride' and the deceptively conventional angels, nuns and madonnas who people Dowson's narratives, undermine, in different ways, the passive womanly ideals in which middle-class culture had, throughout the nineteenth century, invested so much symbolic significance. Dowson delineates, through his unmanly Decadents and resourceful New Women, the contours of new masculine and feminine types, heralding that flexibility and mobility which characterize modern gender roles and identities.

Leonora, the female protagonist of 'An Orchestral Violin' exemplifies the *fin-de-siècle* New Woman. She is a rebellious character who refuses to perform a mere function in her father's fantasy of male power and desire. Far from displaying the silent passivity and inane virtuosity of ideal femininity, Leonora is an articulate and highly-talented *fin-de-siècle* woman. But her aspirations to become an opera singer clash with her father's desires and with larger social designs which conspired to oppress women and restrict their activities to the home. Leonora's search for creative self-expression and artistic realization is seen as being hampered above all by the coercive pressures of patriarchal discourse. The narrating scenario, which features two men alternating in their roles as story tellers, is designed to index a socio-cultural reality where discourse and representation, including representation of the feminine, are exclusively controlled by men. Mr Cristich, Leonora's foster father, and a young bohemian he has befriended in a Soho restaurant decide to tell a story which revolves around their relationship with Leonora. They betray, in the course of their narration, the extent to which the *fin-de-siècle* New Woman, embodied in the protagonist, problematized the power relations between the sexes and precipitated a psychic crisis both in an older and a younger generation of men.

Both as a child, in her relationship with her adoptive father, and as an adult, in her dealings with the young bohemian artist, Leonora is seen as having to conduct a battle for self-expression on the discursive front. Versed from a very early age in the politics of verbal resistance, she refuses to acknowledge her father's authority over her, or submit to his desire to structure her identity according to his needs. Cristich's evocation of an early scene from Leonora's childhood sheds light on the tactics deployed by the little girl to undermine her father's authority and invalidate the oppressive discursive legacy which he, as a patriarchal figurehead, attempts to promote and propagate. Cristich has just scolded Leonora for having stood for hours listening to his music outside his apartment door. He remarks:

> I gave her a kind of scolding, such as one could to so beautiful a little creature, for the passage was draughty and cold, and sent her away with some *bon-bons* (40-41).

Leonora, however, refuses to endorse Cristich's interpretation of reality and appropriating the rhetoric of 'naughtiness', through which the old man attempts to police and regulate her behaviour, she proceeds to fabricate her own version of the truth:

> 'You are not angry, and I am not naughty,' she said: 'and I shall come back. I thank you for your *bon-bons*; but I like your music better than *bon-bons*, or fairy tales, or anything in the world' (41).

Leonora makes it clear that her determination to pursue music will be curbed neither by her father's will, nor his sweets, nor more generally by other manipulative and coercive discourses which, like fairy tales, seek to impart to women a lesson in feminine obedience, silence and passivity.

Confronted by his daughter's rebelliousness, Cristich experiences a crisis. He realizes he has failed to establish absolute control not only over his daughter but also over the word and over the manipulative power of discourse. The lack of control over his daughter entails a loss of power, the power to have the last word and be able to shape his and her destiny according to his needs and desires. The old patriarch is forced to acknowledge defeat:

> I would have kept her with me always but it could not be, from the very first she would be a singer. . . . I held my beautiful, strange bird in her cage, until she beat her wings against the bars, then I opened the door (42-3).

Refusing to have anything to do with Leonora, Cristich determines to punish her by severing his affectionate and economic ties with her. Making one last attempt to strengthen the patriarchal legacy, which he knew his daughter had jeopardized, Cristich disinherits her, leaving his possessions, including a precious Stradivarius, to a man, a bohemian artist he had befriended in a Soho restaurant. Cristich's gesture of male solidarity, however, is lost on this young man who is espoused to the radical politics of the Decadence and is, like Leonora, engaged in a rebellion against the rigid gender roles and oppressive hierarchies perpetrated by the patriarchal system which Cristich embraced and sought to consolidate. Acknowledging the close affinities he had with this young woman and taking into account the 'mixed nature of [his] attraction' (48) to her, the young bohemian determines to defy Cristich's wishes and present Leonora with the violin which the old man had meant him to keep after his death. But the man soon learns that his attempt to establish an alliance with Leonora entails a recognition of the New Woman's sexual and intellectual powers which in turn lead him to experience a crisis in his own sense of masculinity. During the brief but highly-charged exchange he has with Leonora, the young bohemian writer is dumbstruck by her verbal tactics. When they meet for the first time, she responds to his insinuations of filial ingratitude by accusing him of prejudice. She exclaims, alerting him to the malicious gossip to which he has succumbed: 'Oh, you judge me hard, . . . the world busies itself with me, and you are in the lap of its tongues' (48). She then moves from defending her personal integrity to a broader denunciation of female oppression: 'I have paid my penalties', she says, and 'a woman is not free to do as she will' (48). Leonora then proceeds to launch a critique on literary discourse and, addressing the young man's novels, she suggests that he, despite his alleged bohemianism and radicalism, was also responsible for distorting and misrepresenting the feminine. 'I admire your books', she remarks; 'but are your women quite just?' (47) Overwhelmed by Leonora's defence and criticism, the young man is forced to beat a quick retreat. Despite his earlier allegations regarding his attraction to the prima-donna, he cannot help but succumb to fear, the fear imparted by the 'hundred idle stories' which stress Leonora's 'various perversity' (39) and the terror induced in men by the secular misogynistic narratives which equated women's desire for freedom with evil. The young man thus falls prey to fear, and instead of handing the violin to the primadonna in person, as they had agreed, he decides to send it to her through 'the vulgar aid of a *commissionnaire'*(50).

Through this story, Dowson conveys a sense of the volatile power relations between the sexes towards the end of the century. If the older man, posing as patriarch, refuses to recognise his daughter's social and legal rights when he disinherits her, the more radical-minded bohemian attempts a gesture of solidarity and reconciliation when he offers to give Leonora the violin, a symbol of power, self-expression and creativity. The pact that the young man makes with the New Woman, however, is achieved at the cost of a deep psychic wound. The bohemian, who also acts as co-narrator with Cristich, succumbs to mental chaos, as is indexed by his inability to control his plot and bring his narrative to a neat and ordered closure. He ends his story on a precarious note of self-doubt and confusion: 'Have I been pusillanimous, prudent or merely cruel? For the life of me I cannot say' (50).

Again in 'The Eyes of Pride', Dowson mobilizes imagery of strong-willed femininity and unstable masculinity and once more he attempts to convey a sense of the psychic crises that the New Woman precipitated in the *fin-de-siècle* new man. Rosalind Lingard is, like Leonora, a New Woman. We are told that Seefang, her fiancé, has spent several years of his manhood practising Art and engaging, in a Decadent fashion, in 'the frank and unashamed satisfaction of his vigorous appetites' (105). This unmanly and typically Decadent lack of self-restraint propels Seefang towards Rosalind, a 'capricious' woman who did not acknowledge his authority and 'declined to live her life as he would have it' (108). Like the unnamed narrator of 'An Orchestral Violin', Seefang is fascinated by the 'ambiguous charm' and 'adorable imperfection' (105) of this new model of femininity. Yet, not unlike the bohemian narrator of the previous story, he fails to envisage a mode of relating to her outside the structures of power which regulated the traditional heterosexual couple. Seefang thus suffers a masculinity crisis and the two lovers are compelled to break their engagement and go their separate ways.

Seefang's erotic imagination, we are told, fluctuated between his desire for the New Woman embodied in Rosalind, and 'a girl most unlike Rosalind Lingard; a girl with the ambered paleness and the vaguely virginal air of an early Tuscan painting, who would cure him of his grossness and reform him' (105). These Madonna-like ideals of femininity also feature in Dowson's fiction and play a central role in the writer's aesthetic project. In delineating the contours of these virtuous feminine ideals Dowson draws on a rich bourgeois repertoire of household nuns, angels and domesticated Madonnas.[16] Yet, in Dowson's stories, these paragons of virtue undergo a radical transmutation. Instead of performing a function in a bourgeois drama of marriage and procreation, they invariably act as subversive agents undermining the marriage plot and saving themselves and their suitors from sacrificing their individuality and their sexuality to the purposive needs of the community. Marie-Ursule of 'Apple Blossom in Brittany', possesses the unsullied qualities of a Madonna, the innocence of a child, and the vestal purity of a nun. She has, in other words, those characteristics which destined her to occupy the sanctioned niche of mother and wife in the bourgeois household. However, after a brief romantic attachment to her Decadent suitor, she decides to renounce marriage and become a nun instead. Marie-Ursule thus saves both herself and her Decadent admirer from marrying and becoming slaves to 'the vulgarity of instinct, the tyranny of institutions' (98). The subversive implications of Marie-Ursule's decision are voiced by the girl's uncle whose alarm about his niece's decision to abandon matrimony colludes with broader concerns for the future of his nation: 'A vocation, *mon Dieu!* if all the little girls who fancied themselves with one were to have their way, to whom would our poor France look for children?' (94)

Marie-Angèle, in 'Countess Marie of the Angels' is the only female protagonist in Dowson's stories who is not spared from marriage, but this event, the narrative makes explicit, was arranged by a scheming 'iron-featured' grandmother who had resolved that 'the shattered fortunes of a great house . . . were to be retrieved by a rich marriage' (122). Once the heroine's grandmother and husband die, and are safely out of the way, Marie-Angèle takes charge of her life, subverting a course of action which would have led a childhood romance to end in a second marriage. Once more, the female protagonist of this story intercedes on the Decadent Aesthete's behalf, allowing him to make that ultimate sexual 'renunciation' which he regards as 'better than happiness' (130). As for herself, Marie-Angèle chooses to forge a homosocial, non-procreational bond with her daughter. 'You forget I have my child, Ursule', is her timely response to Mallory, when, puzzled by her decision, he expresses concern about her future. By having his angelic ideals reject marriage, Dowson espouses New Woman aesthetics, plotting a course of action for his characters which deliberately undermines conventional romance and its celebraton of heterosexual unions.

Distortions of conventional plot structures, disintegrating forms and disruptive representations of gender and subjectivity collude in Dowson's narratives to stage a show of cultural resistance and ideological subversion. As an emergent 1890s genre, the short story provided Dowson with that flexibility necessary to engage with new narrative techniques and with a platform from which to launch a critique of conventional modes of representation. The short story allowed Dowson to step away from the traditional novel and away from plot structures that he regarded as oppressive, idealistic and decidedly anachronistic.

It is Dowson's short fiction, then, more than his verse, which shows how deeply implicated he was in the politics of resistance and cultural change that characterized the Decadent literary and artistic movement, and it is his fiction which conveys a more vivid sense of the range and complexity of the contribution that Dowson, as an avant-garde writer, made to the *fin-de-siècle* literary movement. Dowson's short stories, with their chaos, their sympathetic representations of Decadent Aesthetes and New Women, their subversion of gender roles and sexuality, provided new cultural alternatives and contributed towards changing the consciousness and drives of the men and women who, in the last decade of the nineteenth century, were aware of the oppressiveness of the world in which they lived and desired to change it.

Notes

1. *The Letters of Ernest Dowson* ed. by Desmond Flower & Henry Maas (London: Cassell, 1967), hereafter referred to as *Letters*. All Dowson scholars are continually grateful for this excellent edition.
2. Dowson told Frank Harris that Poe 'was a master of both prose and verse . . . his prose better than his verse, as mine is'. See Mark Longaker, *The Stories of Ernest Dowson* ed. by Mark Longaker (W.H. Allen: London, 1947), p.1. Longaker's edition is hereafter referred to as *Stories*. See also W. R. Thomas, 'Ernest Dowson at Oxford', *The Nineteenth Century*, April 1928.
3. *Stories*, p. 11.
4. Keith Cushman, 'The Quintessence of Dowsonism: "The Dying of Francis Donne"', *Studies in Short Fiction*, 11 (1974), 45- 51 (45).

5. Chris Snodgrass, 'Aesthetic Memory's Cul-de-sac: The Art of Ernest Dowson', *English Literature in Transition*, 35 (1992), 26-53.

6. Jad Adams, *Madder Music Stronger Wine: The Life of Ernest Dowson, Poet and Decadent* (London, New York: I. B. Tauris, 1999), 17.

7. Mark Longaker remarks that Dowson's stories 'show little integration of character, setting, and plot' and goes on to say that 'they are devoid of real plot, of dramatic development, and stirring action. Furthermore, the characters are generally vague'. *Stories*, 10-11.

8. *Stories*, 4.

9. Dowson here advances an implicit critique against the revival of male romance fiction, a genre which flourished in the last two decades of the century at the hands of Andrew Lang, George Saintsbury, Rider Haggard, G.A. Henty, Robert Louis Stevenson, and Rudyard Kipling. These tales were driven, unlike Dowson's short stories, by the spirit of adventure and the heroic deeds of manly men. For more details on the 1880s revival of the male adventure tale see: Lyn Pykett, *Engendering Fictions: The English Novel in The Early Twentieth Century* (London; New York: Edward Arnold, 1995), 66-69.

10. See Victor Plarr, *Ernest Dowson 1888-1897: Reminiscences, Unpublished Letters and Marginalia* (London: Mathews, 1914), 25.

11. See 'The Dying of Francis Donne', 142 and 143. Further page references to the current edition will be included in the text.

12. Patricia Waugh: *Metafiction: The Theory and Practice of Self-Conscious Fiction* (London: Methuen, 1984).

13. *Stories*, 11.

14. Term used by Herbert Marcuse in *The Aesthetic Dimension: Toward a Critique of Marxist Aesthetics* (London and Basingstoke: Macmillan, 1879). See, in particular, 3-4.

15. *Ibid.*

16. For representations of these ideals in the visual arts, see Bram Dijkstra, *Idols of Perversity: Fantasies of Feminine Evil in Fin-de-Siècle Culture* (New York: Oxford University Press, 1986).

THE DIARY OF A SUCCESSFUL MAN

THE DIARY OF A SUCCESSFUL MAN

1ˢᵗ October, 188 –
Hotel du Lys, Bruges.

After all, few places appeal to my imagination more potently than this autumnal old city – the most mediaeval town in Europe. I am glad that I have come back here at last. It is melancholy indeed, but then at my age one's pleasures are chiefly melancholy. One is essentially of the autumn, and it is always autumn at Bruges. I thought I had been given back my youth when I awoke this morning and heard the Carillon, chiming out, as it has done, no doubt, intermittently, since I heard it last – twenty years ago. Yes, for a moment, I thought I was young again – only for a moment. When I went out into the streets and resumed acquaintance with all my old haunts, the illusion had gone. I strolled into Saint Sauveur's, wandered a while through its dim, dusky aisles, and then sat down near the high altar, where the air was heaviest with stale incense, and indulged in retrospect. I was there for more than an hour. I doubt whether it was quite wise. At my time of life one had best keep out of cathedrals; they are vault-like places, pregnant with rheumatism – at best they are full of ghosts. And a good many *revenants* visited me during that hour of meditation. Afterwards I paid a visit to the Memlings in the Hôpital. Nothing has altered very much; even the women, with their placid, ugly Flemish faces, sitting eternally in their doorways with the eternal lace-pillow, might be the same women. In the afternoon I went to the Béguinage, and sat there long in the shadow of a tree, which must have grown up since my time, I think. I sat there too long, I fear, until the dusk and the chill drove me home to dinner. On the whole perhaps it was a mistake to come back. The sameness of this terribly constant old city seems to intensify the change that has come to oneself. Perhaps if I had come back with Lorimer I should have noticed it less. For, after all, the years have been kind to me, on the whole; they have given me most things which I set my heart upon, and if they had not broken a most perfect friendship, I would forgive them the rest. I sometimes feel, however, that one sacrifices too much to one's success. To slave twenty years at the Indian bar has its drawbacks, even when it does leave one at fifty, prosperous *à mourir d'ennui*. Yes, I must admit that I am prosperous, disgustingly prosperous, and – my wife is dead, and Lorimer – Lorimer has altogether passed out of my life. Ah, it is a mistake to keep a journal – a mistake.

3rd October.

I vowed yesterday that I would pack my portmanteau and move on to Brussels, but to-day finds me still at Bruges. The charm of the old Flemish city grows on me. To-day I carried my peregrinations further a-field. I wandered about the Quais and stood on the old bridge where one obtains such a perfect glimpse, through a trellis of chestnuts, of the red roof and spires of Notre Dame. But the particular locality matters nothing; every nook and corner of Bruges teems with reminiscences. And how fresh they are! At Bombay I had not time to remember or to regret; but to-day the whole dead and forgotten story rises up like a ghost to haunt me. At times, moreover, I have a curious, fantastic feeling, that some day or other, in some mildewing church, I shall come face to face with Lorimer. He was older than I, he must be greatly altered, but I should know him. It is strange how intensely I desire to meet him. I suppose it is chiefly curiosity. I should like to feel sure of him, to explain his silence. He cannot be dead. I am told that he had pictures in this last Academy – and yet, never to have written – never once, through all these years. I suppose there are few friendships which can stand the test of correspondence. Still it is inexplicable, it is not like Lorimer. He could not have harboured a grudge against me – for what? A boyish infatuation for a woman who adored him, and whom he adored. The idea is preposterous, they must have laughed over my folly often, of winter evenings by their fireside. For they married, they must have married, they were made for each other and they knew it. Was their marriage happy I wonder? Was it as successful as mine, though perhaps a little less commonplace? It is strange, though, that I never heard of it, that he never wrote to me once, not through all those years.

4th October.

Inexplicable! Inexplicable! *Did* they marry after all? Could there have been some gigantic misunderstanding? I paid a pilgrimage this morning which hitherto I had deferred, I know not precisely why. I went to the old house in the Rue d'Alva – where she lived, our Comtesse. And the sight of its grim, historic frontal made twenty years seem as yesterday. I meant to content myself with a mere glimpse at the barred windows, but the impulse seized me to ring the bell which I used to ring so often. It was a foolish, fantastic impulse, but I obeyed it. I found it was occupied by an Englishman, a Mr Venables – there seem to be more English here than in my time – and I sent in my card and asked if I might see the famous dining-room. There was no objection raised, my host was most courteous, my name, he said, was familiar to him; he is evidently proud of his dilapidated old palace, and has had the grace to save it from the attentions of the upholsterer. No! twenty years have produced very little change in the room where we had so many pleasant sittings. The ancient stamped leather on the walls is perhaps a trifle more ragged, the old oak panels not blacker – that were im-possible – but a trifle more worm-eaten; it is the same room. I must have seemed a sad boor to my polite cicerone as I stood, hat in hand, and silently took in all the old familiar details. The same smell of mildewed antiquity, I could almost believe the same furniture. And indeed my host tells me that he took over the house as it was, and that some of the chairs and tables are scarcely more youthful than the walls. Yes, there by the huge fireplace was the same quaintly carved chair where she always sat. Ah, those delicious evenings when one was five-and-twenty. For the moment I should not have been surprised if she had suddenly taken shape before my eyes, in the old seat, the slim, girlish woman in her white dress, her hands folded in her lap, her quiet eyes gazing dreamily into the red fire, a subtle air of distinction in her whole posture . . . . . She would be old now, I suppose. Would she? Ah no, she was not one of the women who grow old . . . . . I caught up the thread of my host's discourse just as he was pointing it with a sharp rap upon one of the most time-stained panels.

'Behind there,' he remarked, with pardonable pride, 'is the secret passage where the Due d'Alva was assassinated.'

I smiled apologetically.

'Yes,' I said, 'I know it. I should explain perhaps – my excuse for troubling you was not merely historic curiosity. I have more personal associations with this room. I spent some charming hours in it a great many years ago – ' and for the moment I had forgotten that I was nearly fifty.

'Ah,' he said, with interest, 'you know the late people, the Fontaines.'

'No,' I said, 'I am afraid I have never heard of them. I am very ancient. In my time it belonged to the Savaresse family.'

'So I have heard,' he said, 'but that was long ago. I have only had it a few years. Fontaine my landlord bought it from them. Did you know M. le Comte?'

'No,' I answered, 'Madame la Comtesse. She was left a widow very shortly after her marriage. I never knew M. le Comte.'

My host shrugged his shoulders.

'From all accounts,' he said, 'you did not lose very much.'

'It was an unhappy marriage,' I remarked, vaguely, 'most unhappy. Her second marriage promised greater felicity.'

Mr. Venables looked at me curiously.

'I understood,' he began, but he broke off abruptly. 'I did not know Madame de Savaresse married again.'

His tone had suddenly changed, it had grown less cordial, and we parted shortly afterwards with a certain constraint. And as I walked home pensively curious, his interrupted sentence puzzled me. Does he look upon me as an impostor, a vulgar gossip-monger? What has he heard, what does he know of her? Does he know anything? I cannot help believing so. I almost wish I had asked him definitely, but he would have misunderstood my motives. Yet, even so, I wish I had asked him.

6th October.

I am still living constantly in the past, and the fantastic feeling, whenever I enter a church or turn a corner that I shall meet Lorimer again, has grown into a settled conviction. Yes, I shall meet him, and in Bruges . . . . It is strange how an episode which one has thrust away out of sight and forgotten for years will be started back into renewed life by the merest trifle. And for the last week it has all been as vivid as if it happened yesterday. To-night I have been putting questions to myself – so far with no very satisfactory answer. *Was* it a boyish infatuation after all? Has it passed away as utterly as I believed? I can see her face now as I sit by the fire with the finest precision of detail. I can hear her voice, that soft, low voice, which was none the less sweet for its modulation of sadness. I think there are no women like her now-a-days – none, none! *Did* she marry Lorimer? and if not – ? It seems strange now that we should have both been so attracted, and yet not strange when one considers it. At least we were never jealous of one another. How the details rush back upon one! I think we must have fallen in love with her at the same moment – for we were together when we saw her for the first time, we were together when we went first to call on her in the Rue d'Alva – I doubt if we ever saw her except together. It was soon after we began to get intimate that she wore white again. She told us that we had given her back her youth. She joined our sketching expeditions with the most supreme contempt for *les convenances*; when she was not fluttering round, passing from Lorimer's canvas to mine with her sweetly inconsequent criticism, she sat in the long grass and read to us – André Chénier and Lamartine. In the evening we went to see her; she denied herself to the rest of the world, and we sat for hours in that ancient room in the delicious twilight, while she sang to us – she sang divinely – little French *chansons*, gay and sad, and snatches of *operette*. How we adored her! I think she knew from the first how it would be and postponed it as long as she could. But at last she saw that it was inevitable. . . . I remember the last evening that we were there – remember – shall I ever forget it? We had stayed beyond our usual hour and when we rose to go we all of us knew that those pleasant irresponsible evenings had come to an end. And both Lorimer and I stood for a moment on the threshold before we said good-night, feeling I suppose that one of us was there for the last time.

And how graceful, how gracious she was as she held out one little white hand to Lorimer and one to me. 'Good-night, dear friends,' she said, 'I like you both so much – so much. Believe me, I am grateful to you both – for having given me back my faith in life, in friendship, believe that, will you not, *mes amis*?' Then for just one delirious moment her eyes met mine and it seemed to me – ah, well, after all it was Lorimer she loved.

7th *October.*

It seems a Quixotic piece of folly now, our proposal we would neither take advantage of the other, but we both of us *must* speak. We wrote to her at the same time and likely enough, in the same words, we posted our letters by the same post. To-day I had the curiosity to take out her answer to me from my desk, and I read it quite calmly and dispassionately, the poor yellow letter with the faded ink, which wrote 'Finis' to my youth and made a man of me.

'*Pauvre cher Ami*,' she wrote to me, and when I had read that, for the first time in my life and the only time Lorimer's superiority was bitter to me. The rest I deciphered through scalding tears.

'*Pauvre cher Ami*, I am very sorry for you, and yet I think you should have guessed and have spared yourself this pain, and me too a little. No, my friend, that which you ask of me is impossible. You are my dear friend, but it is your brother whom I love – your brother, for are you not as brothers, and I can not break your beautiful friendship. No, that must not be. See, I ask one favour of you – I have written also to him, only one little word "Viens," – but will you not go to him and tell him for me? Ah, my brother, my heart bleeds for you. I too have suffered in my time. You will go away now, yes, that is best, but you will return when this fancy of yours has passed. Ah forgive me – that I am happy – forgive us, forgive me. Let us still be friends. Adieu! Au revoir.
                                            'Thy Sister,
                                                            'DELPHINE.'

I suppose it was about an hour later that I took out my letter to Lorimer. I told him as I told myself, that it was the fortune of war, that she had chosen the better man, but I could not bear to stay and see their happiness. I was in London before the evening. I wanted work, hard, grinding work, I was tired of being a briefless barrister, and as it happened, an Indian opening offered itself at the very moment when I had decided that Europe had become impossible to me. I accepted it, and so those two happy ones passed out of my life.

Twenty years ago! and in spite of his promise he has never written from that day till this, not so much as a line to tell me of his marriage. I made a vow then that I would get over my folly, and it seemed to me that my vow was kept. And yet here to-day, in Bruges, I am asking myself whether after all it has been such a great success, whether sooner or later one does not have to pay for having been hard and strong, for refusing to suffer. . . . I must leave this place, it is too full of Madame de Savaresse. . . . Is it curiosity which is torturing me? I *must* find Lorimer. If he married her, why has he been so persistently silent? If he did not marry her, what in Heaven's name does it mean? These are vexing questions.

9

10th October.

In the Church of the Dames Rouges, I met to-day my old friend Sebastian Lorimer. Strange! Strange! He was greatly altered, I wonder almost that I recognised him. I had strolled into the church for benediction, for the first time since I have been back here, and when the service was over and I swung back the heavy door, with the exquisite music of the 'O Salutaris,' sung by those buried women behind the screen still echoing in my ear, I paused a moment to let a man pass by me. It was Lorimer, he looked wild and worn; it was no more than the ghost of my old friend. I was shocked and startled by his manner. We shook hands quite impassively as if we had parted yesterday. He talked in a rambling way as we walked towards my hotel, of the singing of the nuns, of the numerous religious processions, of the blessed doctrine of the intercession of saints. The old melodious voice was unchanged, but it was pitched in the singularly low key which I have noticed some foreign priests acquire who live much in churches. I gather that he has become a Catholic. I do not know what intangible instinct, or it may be fear, prevented me from putting to him the vital question which has so perplexed me. It is astonishing how his face has changed, what an extraordinary restlessness his speech and eye have acquired. It never was so of old. My first impression was that he was suffering from some acute form of nervous disorder, but before I left him a more unpleasant suspicion was gradually forced upon me. I cannot help thinking that there is more than a touch of insanity in my old friend. I tried from time to time to bring him down to personal topics, but he eluded them dexterously, and it was only for a moment or so that I could keep him away from the all absorbing subject of the Catholic Church, which seems in some of its more sombre aspects to exercise an extraordinary fascination over him. I asked him if he often visited Bruges.

He looked up at me with a curious expression of surprise.

'I live here,' he said, 'almost always. I have done so for years. . . .' Presently he added hurriedly, 'You have come back. I thought you would come back, but you have been gone a long time – oh, a long time! It seems years since we met. Do you remember – ?' He checked himself; then he added in a low whisper, 'We all come back, we all come back.'

He uttered a quaint, short laugh.

'One can be near – very near, even if one can never be quite close.'

He tells me that he still paints, and that the Academy, to which he sends a picture yearly, has recently elected him an Associate. But his art does not seem to absorb him as it did of old, and he speaks of his success drily and as a matter of very secondary importance. He refused to dine with me, alleging an engagement, but that so hesitatingly and with such vagueness that I could perceive it was the merest pretext. His manner was so strange and remote that I did not venture to press him. I think he is unhappily conscious of his own frequent incoherencies and at moments there are quite painful pauses when he is obviously struggling with dumb piteousness to be lucid, to collect himself and pick up certain lost threads in his memory. He is coming to see me this evening, at his own suggestion, and I am waiting for him now with a strange terror oppressing me. I cannot help thinking that he possesses the key to all that has so puzzled me, and that to-night he will endeavour to speak.

11ᵗʰ October.

Poor Lorimer! I have hardly yet got over the shock which his visit last night caused me, and the amazement with which I heard and read between the lines of his strange confession. His once clear reason is, I fear, hopelessly obscured, and how much of his story is hallucination, I cannot say. His notions of time and place are quite confused, and out of his rambling statement I can only be sure of one fact. It seems that he has done me a great wrong, an irreparable wrong, which he has since bitterly repented.

And in the light of this poor wretch's story, a great misunderstand-ing is rolled away, and I am left with the conviction that the last twenty years have been after all a huge blunder, an irrevocable and miserable mistake. Through my own rash precipitancy and Lorimer's weak treachery, a trivial mischance that a single word would have rectified, has been prolonged beyond hope of redress. It seems that after all it was not Lorimer whom she chose. Madame de Savaresse writing to us both twenty years ago, made a vital and yet not inexplicable mistake. She confused her envelopes, and the letter which I received was never meant for me, although it was couched in such ambiguous terms that until to-day the possibility of this error never dawned on me. And my letter, the one little word of which she spoke, was sent to Lorimer. Poor wretch! he did me a vital injury – yes, I can say that now – a vital injury, but on the whole I pity him. To have been suddenly dashed down from the pinnacles of happiness, it must have been a cruel blow. He tells me that when he saw her that afternoon and found out his mistake, he had no thought except to recall me. He actually came to London for that purpose, having vowed to her solemnly that he would bring me back; it was only in England, that, to use his own distraught phrase, the Devil entered into possession of him. His half-insane ramblings gave me a very vivid idea of that fortnight during which be lay hid in London, trembling like a guilty thing, fearful at every moment that he might run across me and yet half longing for the meeting with the irresoluteness of the weak nature, which can conceive and to a certain extent execute a *lâcheté*, yet which would always gladly yield to circumstance and let chance or fate decide the issue. And to the very last Lorimer was wavering – had almost sought me out, and thrown himself on my mercy, when the news came that I had sailed.

Destiny, who has no weak scruples, had stepped in and sealed Delphine's mistake for all time, after her grim fashion. When he went back to Bruges, and saw Madame de Savaresse, I think she must have partly guessed his baseness. Lorimer was not strong enough to be a successful hypocrite, and that meeting, I gather, was also their final parting. She must have said things to him in her beautiful quiet voice which he has never forgotten. He went away and each day he was going to write to me, and each day he deferred it, and then he took up the *Times* one morning and read the announcement of my marriage. After that it seemed so him that he could only be silent. . . .

Did *she* know of it too? Did she suffer or did she understand? Poor woman! poor woman! I wonder if she consoled herself, as I did, and if so how she looks back on her success? I wonder whether she is happy, whether she is dead? I suppose these are questions which will remain unanswered. And yet when Lorimer left me at a late hour last night, it seemed to me that the air was full of unspoken words. Does he know anything of her now! I have a right to ask him these things. And to-morrow I am to meet him, he made the request most strangely – at the same place where we fell in with each other to-day – until to-morrow then!

12th October.

I have just left Sebastian Lorimer at the Church of the Dames Rouges. I hope I was not cruel, but there are some things which one can neither forget nor forgive, and it seemed to me that when I knew the full measure of the ruin he had wrought, my pity for him withered away. 'I hope, Lorimer,' I said, 'that we may never meet again.' And, honestly, I can not forgive him. If she had been happy, if she had let time deal gently with her – ah yes, even if she were dead – it might be easier. But that this living entombment, this hopeless death in life should befall her, she so magnificently fitted for life's finer offices, ah, the pity of it, the pity of it! . . . . But let me set down the whole sad story as it dawned upon me this afternoon in that unearthly church. I was later than the hour appointed; vespers were over and a server, taper in hand, was gradually transforming the gloom of the high altar into a blaze of light. With a strange sense of completion I took my place next to the chair by which Lorimer, with bowed head, was kneeling, his eyes fixed with a strange intentness on the screen which separated the outer worshippers from the chapel or gallery which was set apart for the nuns. His lips moved from time to time spasmodically, in prayer or ejaculation: then as the jubilant organ burst out, and the officiating priest in his dalmatic of cloth of gold passed from the sacristy and genuflected at the altar, he seemed to be listening in a very passion of attention. But as the incense began to fill the air, and the Litany of Loreto smote on my ear to some sorrowful, undulating Gregorian, I lost thought of the wretched man beside me; I forgot the miserable mistake that he had perpetuated, and I was once more back in the past – with Delphine – kneeling by her side. Strophe by strophe that perfect litany rose and was lost in a cloud of incense, in the mazy arches of the roof.

> 'Janua cœli,
> Stella matutina,
> Salus infirmorum, Ora pro nobis!'

Instrophe and antistrophe: the melancholy, nasal intonation of the priest died away, and the exquisite women's voices in the gallery took it up with exultation, and yet with something like a sob – a sob of limitation.

> 'Refugium peccatorum,
> Consolatrix afflictorum,
> Auxilium Christianorum, Ora pro nobis!'

And so on through all the exquisite changes of the hymn, until the time of the music changed, and the priest intoned the closing line.

> 'Ora pro nobis, Sancta Dei Genetrix!'

and the voices in the gallery answered:

> 'Ut digni efficiamur promissionibus Christi.'

There was one voice which rose above all the others, a voice of marvellous sweetness and power, which from the first moment had caused me a curious thrill. And presently Lorimer bent down and whispered to me: 'So near,' he murmured, 'and yet so far away – so near, and yet never quite close!'

But before he had spoken I had read in his rigid face, in his eyes fixed with such a passion of regret on the screen, why we were there – whose voice it was we had listened to.

I rose and went out of the church quietly and hastily; I felt that to stay there one moment longer would be suffocation. . . Poor woman! so this is how she sought consolation, in religion! Well, there are different ways for different persons – and for me – what is there left for me? Oh, many things, no doubt, many things. Still, for once and for the last time, let me set myself down as a dreary fraud. I never forgot her, not for one hour or day, not even when it seemed to me that I had forgotten her most, not even when I married. No woman ever represented to me the same idea as Madame de Savaresse. No woman's voice was ever sweet to me after hers, the touch of no woman's hand ever made my heart beat one moment quicker for pleasure or for pain, since I pressed hers for the last time on that fateful evening twenty years ago. Even so – ! . . .

When the service was over and the people had streamed out and dispersed, I went back for the last time into the quiet church. A white robed server was extinguishing the last candle on the altar; only the one red light perpetually vigilant before the sanctuary, made more visible the deep shadows everywhere.

Lorimer was still kneeling with bowed head in his place. Presently he rose and came towards me. 'She was there – Delphine – you heard her. Ah, Dion, she loves you, she always loves you, you are avenged.'

I gather that for years he has spent hours daily in this church, to be near her, and hear her voice, the magnificent voice rising above all the other voices in the chants of her religion. But he will never see her, for is she not of the Dames Rouges? And I remember now all the stories of the Order, of its strictness, its austerity, its perfect isolation. And chiefly, I remember how they say that only twice after one of these nuns has taken her vows is she seen of anyone except those of her community; once, when she enters the Order, the door of the convent is thrown back and she is seen for a single moment in the scarlet habit of the Order, by the world, by all who care to gaze; and once more, at the last, when clad in the same coarse red garb, they bear her out quietly, in her coffin, into the church.

And of this last meeting, Lorimer, I gather, is always restlessly expectant, his whole life concentrated, as it were, in a very passion of waiting for a moment which will surely come. His theory, I confess, escapes me, nor can I guess how far a certain feverish remorse, an intention of expiation may be set as a guiding spring in his unhinged mind, and account, at least in part, for the fantastic attitude which he must have adopted for many years. If I cannot forgive him, at least I bear him no malice, and for the rest, our paths will hardly cross again. One takes up one's life and expiates its errors, each after one's several fashion – and my way is not Lorimer's. And now that it is all so clear, there is nothing to keep me here any longer, nothing to bring me back again. For it seemed to me to-day, strangely enough, as though a certain candle of hope, of promise, of pleasant possibilities, which had flickered with more or less light for so many years, had suddenly gone out and left me alone in utter darkness, as the knowledge was borne in upon me that henceforth Madame de Savaresse had passed altogether and finally out of my life.

And so to-morrow – Brussels!

A CASE OF CONSCIENCE

A CASE OF CONSCIENCE

I

It was in Brittany, and the apples were already acquiring a ruddier, autumnal tint, amid their greens and yellows, though Autumn was not yet; and the country lay very still and fair in the sunset which had befallen, softly and suddenly as is the fashion there. A man and a girl stood looking down in silence at the village, Ploumariel, from their post of vantage, half way up the hill: at its lichened church spire, dotted with little gables, like dove-cotes; at the slated roof of its market; at its quiet white houses. The man's eyes rested on it complacently, with the enjoyment of the painter, finding it charming: the girl's, a little absently, as one who had seen it very often before. She was pretty and very young, but her gray serious eyes, the poise of her head, with its rebellious brown hair braided plainly, gave her a little air of dignity, of reserve which sat piquantly upon her youth. In one ungloved hand, that was brown from the sun, but very beautiful, she held an old parasol, the other played occasionally with a bit of purple heather. Presently she began to speak, using English just coloured by a foreign accent, that made her speech prettier.

'You make me afraid,' she said, turning her large, troubled eyes on her companion, 'you make me afraid, of myself chiefly, but a little of

19

you. You suggest so much to me that is new, strange, terrible. When you speak, I am troubled; all my old landmarks appear to vanish; I even hardly know right from wrong. I love you, my God, how I love you! but I want to go away from you and pray in the little quiet church, where I made my first Communion. I will come to the world's end with you: but oh; Sebastian, do not ask me, let me go. You will forget me, I am a little girl to you Sebastian. You cannot care very much for me.'

The man looked down at her, smiling masterfully, but very kindly. He took the mutinous hand, with its little sprig of heather, and held it between his own. He seemed to find her insistence adorable; mentally, he was contrasting her with all other women whom he had known, frowning at the memory of so many years in which she had no part. He was a man of more than forty, built large to an uniform English pattern; there was a touch of military erectness in his carriage which often deceived people as to his vocation. Actually, he had never been anything but artist, though he came of a family of soldiers, and had once been war correspondent of an illustrated paper. A certain distinction had always adhered to him, never more than now when he was no longer young, was growing bald, had streaks of gray in his moustache. His face, without being handsome, possessed a certain charm; it was worn and rather pale, the lines about the firm mouth were full of lassitude, the eyes rather tired. He had the air of having tasted widely, curiously, of life in his day, prosperous as he seemed now, that had left its mark upon him. His voice, which usually took an intonation that his friends found supercilious, grew very tender in addressing this little French girl, with her quaint air of childish dignity.

'Marie-Yvonne, foolish child, I will not hear one word more. You are a little heretic; and I am sorely tempted to seal your lips from uttering heresy. You tell me that you love me, and you ask me to let you go, in one breath. The impossible conjuncture! Marie-Yvonne,' he added, more seriously, 'trust yourself to me, my child! You know, I will never give you up. You know that these months that I have been at Ploumariel, are worth all the rest of my life to me. It has been a difficult life, hitherto, little one: change it for me; make it worth while. You would let morbid fancies come between us. You have lived overmuch in that little church, with its worm-eaten benches, and its mildewed odour of dead people, and dead ideas. Take care, Marie-Yvonne: it has made you serious-eyed, before you have learnt to laugh; by and by, it will steal away your youth, before you have ever been young. I come to claim you, Marie-Yvonne, in the name of Life.' His words were half-jesting; his eyes were profoundly in earnest. He drew her to him gently; and when he bent down and kissed her forehead, and then her shy lips, she made no resistance: only, a little tremor ran through her. Presently, with equal gentleness, he put her away from him. 'You have already given me your answer, Marie-Yvonne. Believe me, you will never regret it. Let us go down.'

They took their way in silence towards the village; presently a bend of the road hid them from it, and he drew closer to her, helping her with his arm over the rough stones. Emerging, they had gone thirty yards so, before the scent of English tobacco drew their attention to a figure seated by the road-side, under a hedge; they recognised it, and started apart, a little consciously.

'It is M. Tregellan,' said the young girl, flushing: 'and he must have seen us.'

Her companion, frowning, hardly suppressed a little quick objurgation.

'It makes no matter,' he observed, after a moment: 'I shall see your uncle to-morrow and we know, good man, how he wishes this; and, in any case, I would have told Tregellan.'

The figure rose, as they drew near: he shook the ashes out of his briar, and removed it to his pocket. He was a slight man, with an ugly, clever face; his voice as he greeted them, was very low and pleasant.

'You must have had a charming walk, Mademoiselle. I have seldom seen Ploumariel look better.'

'Yes,' she said, gravely, 'it has been very pleasant. But I must not linger now,' she added breaking a little silence in which none of them seemed quite at ease. 'My uncle will be expecting me to supper.' She held out her hand, in the English fashion, to Tregellan, and then to Sebastian Murch; who gave the little fingers a private pressure.

They had come into the market-place round which most of the houses in Ploumariel were grouped. They watched the young girl cross it briskly; saw her blue gown pass out of sight down a bye street: then they turned to their own hotel. It was a low, white house, belted half way down the front with black stone; a pictorial object, as most Breton hostels. The ground floor was a *café*; and, outside it, a bench and long stained table enticed them to rest. They sat down, and ordered *absinthes*, as the hour suggested: these were brought to them presently by an old servant of the house; an admirable figure, with the white sleeves and apron relieving her linsey dress: with her good Breton face, and its effective wrinkles. For some time they sat in silence, drinking and smoking. The artist appeared to be absorbed in contemplation of his drink; considering its clouded green in various lights. After a while the other looked up, and remarked, abruptly.

'I may as well tell you that I happened to overlook you, just now, unintentionally.'

Sebastian Murch held up his glass, with absent eyes.

'Don't mention it, my dear fellow,' he remarked, at last, urbanely.

'I beg your pardon; but I am afraid I must.'

He spoke with an extreme deliberation, which suggested nervousness; with the air of a person reciting a little set speech, learnt imperfectly: and he looked very straight in front of him, out into the street, at two dogs quarrelling over some offal.

'I daresay you will be angry: I can't avoid that; at least, I have known you long enough to hazard it. I have had it on my mind to say something. If I have been silent, it hasn't been because I have been blind, or approved. I have seen how it was all along. I gathered it from your letters when I was in England. Only until this afternoon I did not know how far it had gone, and now I am sorry I did not speak before.'

He stopped short, as though he expected his friend's subtilty to come to his assistance; with admissions or recriminations. But the other was still silent, absent: his face wore a look of annoyed indifference. After a while, as Tregellan still halted, he observed quietly:

'You must be a little more explicit. I confess I miss your meaning.'

'Ah, don't be paltry,' cried the other, quickly. 'You know my meaning. To be very plain, Sebastian, are you quite justified in playing with that charming girl, in compromising her?'

The artist looked up at last, smiling: his expressive mouth was set, not angrily, but with singular determination.

'With Mademoiselle Mitouard?'

'Exactly; with the niece of a man whose guest you have recently been.'

'My dear fellow!' he stopped a little, considering his words: 'You are hasty and uncharitable for such a very moral person! you jump at conclusions, Tregellan. I don't, you know, admit your right to question me: still, as you have introduced the subject, I may as well satisfy you. I have asked Mademoiselle Mitouard to marry me, and she has consented, subject to her uncle's approval. And that her uncle, who happens to prefer the English method of courtship, is not likely to refuse.'

The other held his cigar between two fingers, a little away; his curiously anxious face suggested that the question had become to him one of increased nicety.

'I am sorry,' he said, after a moment; 'this is worse than I imagined; it's impossible.'

'It is you that are impossible, Tregellan,' said Sebastian Murch. He looked at him now, quite frankly, absolutely: his eyes had a defiant light in them, as though he hoped to be criticised; wished nothing better than to stand on his defence, to argue the thing out. And Tregellan sat for a long time without speaking, appreciating his purpose. It seemed more monstrous the closer he considered it: natural enough withal, and so, harder to defeat; and yet, he was sure, that defeated it must be. He reflected how accidental it had all been: their presence there, in Ploumariel, and the rest! Touring in Brittany, as they had often done before, in their habit of old friends, they had fallen upon it by chance, a place unknown of Murray; and the merest chance had held them there.

They had slept at the *Lion d'Or*, voted it magnificently picturesque, and would have gone away and forgotten it; but the chance of travel had for once defeated them. Hard by they heard of the little votive chapel of Saint Bernard; at the suggestion of their hostess they set off to visit it. It was built steeply on an edge of rock, amongst odorous pines overhanging a ravine, at the bottom of which they could discern a brown torrent purling tumidly along. For the convenience of devotees, iron rings, at short intervals, were driven into the wall; holding desperately to these, the pious pilgrim, at some peril, might compass the circuit; saying an oraison to Saint Bernard, and some ten *Aves*. Sebastian, who was charmed with the wild beauty of the scene, in a country ordinarily so placid, had been seized with a fit of emulation: not in any mood of devotion, but for the sake of a wider prospect. Tregellan had protested: and the Saint, resenting the purely æsthetic motive of the feat, had seemed to intervene. For, half-way round, growing giddy may be, the artist had made a false step, lost his hold. Tregellan, with a little cry of horror, saw him disappear amidst crumbling mortar and uprooted ferns. It was with a sensible relief, for the fall had the illusion of great depth, that, making his way rapidly down a winding path, he found him lying on a grass terrace, amidst *débris* twenty feet lower, cursing his folly, and holding a lamentably sprained ankle, but for the rest uninjured! Tregellan had made off in haste to Ploumariel in search of assistance; and within the hour he had returned with two stalwart Bretons and M. le Docteur Mitouard.

Their tour had been, naturally, drawing to its close. Tregellan indeed had an imperative need to be in London within the week. It seemed, therefore, a clear dispensation of Providence, that the amiable doctor should prove an hospitable person, and one inspiring confidence no less. Caring greatly for things foreign, and with an especial passion for England, a country whence his brother had brought back a wife, M. le Docteur Mitouard insisted that the invalid could be cared for properly at his house alone. And there, in spite of protestations, earnest from Sebastian, from Tregellan half-hearted, he was installed. And there, two days later, Tregellan left him with an easy mind; bearing away with him, half enviously, the recollection of the young, charming face of a girl, the Doctor's niece, as he had seen her standing by his friend's sofa when he paid his *adieux*; in the beginnings of an intimacy, in which, as he foresaw, the petulance of the invalid, his impatience at an enforced detention, might be considerably forgot. And all that had been two months ago.

II

'1 am sorry you don't see it,' continued Tregellan, after a pause, 'to me it seems impossible; considering your history it takes me by surprise.'

The other frowned slightly; finding this persistence perhaps a trifle crude, he remarked good-humouredly enough:

'Will you be good enough to explain your position? Do you object to the girl? You have been back a week now, during which you have seen almost as much of her as I.'

'She is a child, to begin with; there is five-and-twenty years' disparity between you. But it's the relation I object to, not the girl. Do you intend to live in Ploumariel?'

Sebastian smiled, with a suggestion of irony.

'Not precisely; I think it would interfere a little with my career; why do you ask?'

'I imagined not; you will go back to London with your little Breton wife, who is as charming here as the apple-blossom in her own garden. You will introduce her to your circle, who will receive her with open arms; all the clever bores, who write, and talk, and paint, and are talked about between Bloomsbury and Kensington. Everybody who is emancipated will know her, and everybody who has a "fad"; and they will come in a body and emancipate her, and teach her their "fads."'

'That is a caricature of my circle, as you call it, Tregellan! though I may remind you it is also yours. I think she is being starved in this corner, spiritually. She has a beautiful soul, and it has had no chance. I propose to give it one, and I am not afraid of the result.'

Tregellan threw away the stump of his cigar into the darkling street, with a little gesture of discouragement, of lassitude.

'She has had the chance to become what she is, a perfect thing.'

'My dear fellow,' exclaimed his friend, 'I could not have said more myself.'

The other continued, ignoring his interruption.

'She has had great luck. She has been brought up by an old eccentric, on the English system of growing up as she liked. And no harm has come of it, at least until it gave you the occasion of making love to her.'

'You are candid, Tregellan!'

'Let her go, Sebastian, let her go,' he continued, with increasing gravity. 'Consider what a transplantation; from this world of Ploumariel where everything is fixed for her by that venerable old *Curé*, where life is so easy, so ordered, to yours, ours; a world without definitions, where everything is an open question.'

'Exactly,' said the artist, 'why should she be so limited? I would give her scope, ideas. I can't see that I am wrong.'

'She will not accept them, your ideas. They will trouble her, terrify her; in the end, divide you. It is not an elastic nature. I have watched it.'

'At least, allow me to know her,' put in the artist, a little grimly.

Tregellan shook his head.

'The Breton blood; her English mother: passionate Catholicism! a touch of Puritan! Have you quite made up your mind, Sebastian?'

'I made it up long ago, Tregellan!'

The other looked at him, curiously, compassionately; with a touch of resentment at what he found his lack of subtilty. Then he said at last:

'I called it impossible: you force me to be very explicit, even cruel. I must remind you, that you are, of all my friends, the one I value most, could least afford to lose.'

'You must be going to say something extremely disagreeable! something horrible,' said the artist, slowly.

'I am,' said Tregellan, 'but I must say it. Have you explained to

Mademoiselle, or her uncle, your – your peculiar position?'

Sebastian was silent for a moment, frowning: the lines about his mouth grew a little sterner; as last he said coldly:

'If I were to answer, Yes?'

'Then I should understand that there was no further question of your marriage.'

Presently the other commenced in a hard, leaden voice.

'No, I have not told Marie-Yvonne that. I shall not tell her. I have suffered enough for a youthful folly; an act of mad generosity. I refuse to allow an infamous woman to wreck my future life as she has disgraced my past. Legally, she has passed out of it; morally, legally, she is not my wife. For all I know she may he actually dead.'

The other was watching his face, very gray and old now, with an anxious compassion.

'You know she is not dead, Sebastian,' he said simply. Then he added very quietly as one breaks supreme bad tidings, 'I must tell you something which I fear you have not realised. The Catholic Church does not recognise divorce. If she marry you and find out, rightly or wrongly she will believe that she has been living in sin; some day she will find it out. No damnable secret like that keeps itself for ever: an old newspaper, a chance remark from one of your dear friends, and, the deluge. Do you see the tragedy, the misery of it? By God, Sebastian, to save you both somebody shall tell her; and if it be not you, it must be I.'

There was extremest peace in the quiet square; the houses seemed sleepy as last, after a day of exhausting tranquillity, and the chestnuts, under which a few children, with tangled hair and fair dirty faces, still played. The last glow of the sun fell on the gray roofs opposite; dying hard it seemed over the street in which the Mitouards lived; and they heard suddenly the tinkle of an *Angelus* bell. Very placid! the place and the few peasants in their pictorial hats and caps who lingered. Only the two Englishmen sitting, their glasses empty, and their smoking over, looking out on it all with their anxious faces, brought in a contrasting note of modern life; of the complex aching life of cities, with its troubles and its difficulties.

'Is that your final word, Tregellan?' asked the artist at last, a little wearily.

'It must be, Sebastian! Believe me, I am infinitely sorry.'

'Yes, of course,' he answered quickly, acidly; 'well, I will sleep on it.'

III

They made their first breakfast in an almost total silence; both wore the bruised harassed air which tells of a night passed without benefit of sleep. Immediately afterwards Murch went out alone: Tregellan could guess the direction of his visit, but not its object; he wondered if the artist was making his difficult confession. Presently they brought him in a pencilled note; he recognised, with some surprise, his friend's tortuous hand.

'I have considered our conversation, and your unjustifiable interference. I am entirely in your hands: at the mercy of your extraordinary notions of duty. Tell her what you will, if you must; and pave the way to your own success. I shall say nothing; but I swear you love the girl yourself; and are no right arbiter here. Sebastian Murch.'

He read the note through twice before he grasped its purport; then sat holding it in lax fingers, his face grown singularly gray.

'It's not true, it's not true,' he cried aloud, but a moment later knew himself for a self-deceiver all along. Never had self-consciousness been more sudden, unexpected, or complete. There was no more to do or say; this knowledge tied his hands. *Ite! missa est!* . . .

He spent an hour painfully invoking casuistry, tossed to and fro irresolutely, but never for a moment disputing that plain fact which Sebastian had so brutally illuminated. Yes! he loved her, had loved her all along. Marie-Yvonne! how the name expressed her! at once sweet and serious, arch and sad as her nature. The little Breton wild flower! how cruel it seemed to gather her! And he could do no more; Sebastian had tied his hands. Things must be! He was a man nicely conscientious, and now all the elaborate devices of his honour, which had persuaded him to a disagreeable interference, were contraposed against him. This suspicion of an ulterior motive had altered it, and so at last he was left to decide with a sigh, that because he loved these two so well, he must let them go their own way to misery.

Coming in later in the day, Sebastian Murch found his friend packing.

'I have come to get your answer,' he said; 'I have been walking about the hills like a madman for hours. I have not been near her; I am afraid. Tell me what you mean to do?'

Tregellan rose, shrugged his shoulders, pointed to his valise.

'God help you both! I would have saved you if you had let me. The Quimperlé *Courrier* passes in half-an-hour. I am going by it. I shall catch a night train to Paris.'

As Sebastian said nothing; continued to regard him with the same dull, anxious gaze, he went on after a moment:

'You did me a grave injustice; you should have known me better than that. God knows I meant nothing shameful, only the best; the least misery for you and her.'

'It was true then?' said Sebastian, curiously. His voice was very cold; Tregellan found him altered. He regarded the thing as if it had been very remote, and outside them both.

'I did not know it then,' said Tregellan, shortly.

He knelt down again and resumed his packing. Sebastian, leaning against the bed, watched him with absent intensity, which was yet alive to trivial things, and he handed him from time to time a book, a brush, which the other packed mechanically with elaborate care. There was no more to say, and presently, when the chambermaid entered for his luggage, they went down and out into the splendid sunshine, silently. They had to cross the Square to reach the carriage, a dusty ancient vehicle, hooded, with places for four, which waited outside the post-office. A man in a blue blouse preceded them, carrying Tregellan's things. From the corner they could look down the road to Quimperlé, and their eyes both sought the white house of Doctor Mitouard, standing back a little in its trim garden, with its one incongruous apple tree; but there was no one visible.

Presently, Sebastian asked, suddenly:

'Is it true, that you said last night: divorce to a Catholic – ?'

Tregellan interrupted him.

'It is absolutely true, my poor friend.'

He had climbed into his place at the back, settled himself on the shiny leather cushion: he appeared to be the only passenger. Sebastian stood looking drearily in at the window, the glass of which had long perished.

'I wish I had never known, Tregellan! How could I ever tell her!'

Inside, Tregellan shrugged his shoulders: not impatiently, or angrily, but in sheer impotence; as one who gave it up.

'I can't help you,' he said, 'you must arrange it with your own conscience.'

'Ah, it's too difficult!' cried the other: 'I can't find my way.'

The driver cracked his whip, suggestively; Sebastian drew back a little further from the off wheel.

'Well,' said the other, 'if you find it, write and tell me. I am very sorry, Sebastian.'

'Good-bye,' he replied. 'Yes! I will write.'

The carriage lumbered off, with a lurch to the right, as it turned the corner; it rattled down the hill, raising a cloud of white dust. As it passed the Mitouards' house, a young girl, in a large straw hat, came down the garden; too late to discover whom it contained. She watched it out of sight, indifferently, leaning on the little iron gate; then she turned, to recognise the long stooping figure of Sebastian Murch, who advanced to meet her.

AN ORCHESTRAL VIOLIN

AN ORCHESTRAL VIOLIN

I

At my dining-place in old Soho – I call it mine because there was a time when I became somewhat inveterate there, keeping my napkin (changed once a week) in a ring recognisable by myself and the waiter, my bottle of Beaune (replenished more frequently), and my accustomed seat – at this restaurant of mine, with its confusion of tongues, its various, foreign *clientèle*, amid all the coming and going, the nightly change of faces, there were some which remained the same, persons with whom, though one might never have spoken, one had nevertheless from the mere continuity of juxtaposition a certain sense of intimacy.

There was one old gentleman in particular, as inveterate as myself, who especially aroused my interest. A courteous, punctual, mild old man with an air which deprecated notice; who conversed each evening for a minute or two with the proprietor, as he rolled, always at the same hour, a valedictory cigarette, in a language that arrested my ear by its strangeness; and which proved to be his own, Hungarian; who addressed a brief remark to me at times, half apologetically, in the precisest of English. We sat next each other at the same table, came and went at much the same hour; and for a long while our intercourse was

restricted to formal courtesies; mutual inquiries after each other"s
health, a few urbane strictures on the climate. The little old gentleman
in spite of his aspect of shabby gentility, – for his coat was sadly
inefficient, and the nap of his carefully brushed hat did not indicate
prosperity – perhaps even because of this suggestion of fallen fortunes,
bore himself with pathetic erectness, almost haughtily. He did not seem
amenable to advances. It was a long time before I knew him well enough
to value rightly this appearance, the timid defences, behind which a
very shy and delicate nature took refuge from the world's coarse
curiosity. I can smile now, with a certain sadness, when I remind myself
that at one time I was somewhat in awe of M. Maurice Cristich and his
little air of proud humility. Now that his place in that dim, foreign
eating-house knows him no more, and his yellow napkin-ring, with its
distinguishing number, has been passed on to some other customer; I
have it in my mind to set down my impressions of him, the short history
of our acquaintance. It began with an exchange of cards; a form to which
he evidently attached a ceremonial value, for after that piece of ritual
his manner underwent a sensible softening, and he showed by many
subtle indefinable shades in his courteous address, that he did me the
honour of including me in his friendship. I have his card before me
now; a large, oblong piece of pasteboard, with *M. Maurice Cristich,
Theatre Royal*, inscribed upon it, amid many florid flourishes. It enabled
me to form my first definite notion of his calling, upon which I had
previously wasted much conjecture; though I had all along, and rightly
as it appeared, associated him in some manner with music.

In time he was good enough to inform me further. He was a
musician, a violinist; and formerly, and in his own country, he had
been a composer. But whether for some lack in him of original talent,
or of patience, whether for some grossness in the public taste, on which
the nervous delicacy and refinement of his execution was lost, he had
not continued. He had been driven by poverty to London, had given
lessons, and then for many years had played a second violin in the
orchestra of the Opera.

'It is not much, Monsieur!' he observed, deprecatingly, smoothing his hat with the cuff of his frayed coat-sleeve. 'But it is sufficient; and I prefer it to teaching. In effect, they are very charming, the seraphic young girls of your country! But they seem to care little for music; and I am a difficult master, and have not enough patience. Once, you see, a long time ago, I had a perfect pupil, and perhaps that spoilt me. Yes! I prefer the theatre, though it is less profitable. It is not as it once was,' he added, with a half sigh; 'I am no longer ambitious. Yes, Monsieur, when I was young, I was ambitious. I wrote a symphony and several concertos. I even brought out at Vienna an opera, which I thought would make me famous; but the good folk of Vienna did not appreciate me, and they would have none of my music. They said it was antiquated, my opera, and absurd; and yet, it seemed to me good. I think that Gluck, that great genius, would have liked it; and that is what I should have wished. Ah! how long ago it seems, that time when I was ambitious! But you must excuse me, Monsieur! your good company makes me garrulous. I must be at the theatre. If I am not in my place at the half-hour, they fine me two shillings and sixpence, and that I can ill afford, you know, Monsieur!'

In spite of his defeats, his long and ineffectual struggle with adversity, M. Cristich, I discovered, as our acquaintance ripened, had none of the spleen and little of the vanity of the unsuccessful artist. He seemed in his forlorn old age to have accepted his discomfiture with touching resignation, having acquired neither cynicism nor indifference. He was simply an innocent old man, in love with his violin and with his art, who had acquiesced in disappointment; and it was impossible to decide, whether he even believed in his talent, or had not silently accredited the verdict of musical Vienna, which had condemned his opera in those days when he was ambitious. The precariousness of the London Opera was the one fact which I ever knew to excite him to expressions of personal resentment. When its doors were closed, his hard poverty (it was the only occasion when he protested against it), drove him, with his dear instrument and his accomplished fingers, into the orchestras of lighter houses, where he was compelled to play music which he despised. He grew silent and rueful during these periods of irksome servitude, rolled innumerable cigarettes, which he smoked with fierce-ness and great rapidity. When dinner was done, he was often volubly indignant, in Hungarian, to the proprietor. But with the beginning of the season his mood lightened. He bore himself more sprucely, and would leave me, to assist at a representation of *Don Giovanni*, or *Tann-hauser*, with a face which was almost radiant. I had known him a year before it struck me that I should like to see him in his professional capacity. I told him of my desire a little diffidently, not knowing how my purpose might strike him. He responded graciously, but with an air of intrigue, laying a gentle hand upon my coat sleeve and bidding me wait. A day or two later, as we sat over our coffee, M. Cristich with an hesitating urbanity offered me an order.

'If you would do me the honour to accept it, Monsieur! It is a stall, and a good one! I have never asked for one before, all these years, so they gave it to me easily. You see, I have few friends. It is for to-morrow, as you observe. I demanded it especially; it is an occasion of great inter-est to me – ah! an occasion! You will come?'

'You are too good, M. Cristich!' I said with genuine gratitude, for indeed the gift came in season, the opera being at that time a luxury I could seldom command. 'Need I say that I shall be delighted? And to hear Madame Romanoff, a chance one has so seldom!'

The old gentleman's mild, dull eyes glistened. 'Madame Rcmanoff!' he repeated, 'the marvellous Leonora! yes, yes! She has sung only once before in London. Ah, when I remember – ' He broke off suddenly. As he rose, and prepared for departure, he held my hand a little longer than usual, giving it a more intimate pressure.

'My dear young friend, will you think me a presumptuous old man, if I ask you to come and see me to-morrow in my apartment, when it is over? I will give you a glass of whisky, and we will smoke pipes, and you shall tell me your impressions – and then I will tell you why to-morrow I shall be so proud, why I show this emotion.'

II

The Opera was *Fidelio*, that stately, splendid work, whose melody, if one may make a pictorial comparison, has something of that rich and sun-warm colour which, certainly, on the canvases of Rubens, affects one as an almost musical quality. It offered brilliant opportunities, and the incomparable singer had wasted none of them. So that when, at last, I pushed my way out of the crowded house and joined M. Cristich at the stage door, where he waited with eyes full of expectancy, the music still lingered about me, like the faint, past fragrance of incense, and I had no need to speak my thanks. He rested a light hand on my arm, and we walked towards his lodging silently; the musician carrying his instrument in its sombre case, and shivering from time to time, a tribute to the keen spring night. He stopped as he walked, his eyes trailing the ground; and a certain listlessness in his manner struck me a little strangely, as though he came fresh from some solemn or hieratic experience, of which the reaction had already begun to set in tediously, leaving him at the last unstrung and jaded, a little weary, of himself and the too strenuous occasion. It was not until we had crossed the threshold of a dingy, high house in a byway of Bloomsbury, and he had ushered me, with apologies, into his shabby room, near the sky, that the sense of his hospitable duties seemed to renovate him.

He produced tumblers from an obscure recess behind his bed; set a kettle on the fire, a lodging-house fire, which scarcely smouldered with flickers of depressing, sulphurous flame, talking of indifferent subjects, as he watched for it to boil.

Only when we had settled ourselves, in uneasy chairs, opposite each other, and he had composed me, what he termed 'a grog': himself preferring the more innocent mixture known as *eau sucrée*, did he allude to *Fidelio*. I praised heartily the discipline of the orchestra, the prima donna, whom report made his country-woman, with her strong, sweet voice and her extraordinary beauty, the magnificence of the music, the fine impression of the whole.

M. Cristich, his glass in hand, nodded approval. He looked intently into the fire, which cast mocking shadows over his quaint, incongruous figure, his antiquated dress coat, which seemed to skimp him, his frost-bitten countenance, his cropped gray hair. 'Yes,' he said, 'Yes! So it pleased you, and you thought her beautiful? I am glad.'

He turned round to me abruptly, and laid a thin hand impressively on my knee.

'You know I invented her, the Romanoff, discovered her, taught her all she learnt. Yes, Monsieur, I was proud to-night, very proud, to be there, playing for her, though she did not know. Ah! the beautiful creature! . . . and how badly I played! execrably! You could not notice that, Monsieur, but they did, my *confrères*, and could not understand. How should they? How should they dream, that I, Maurice Cristich, second violin in the orchestra of the opera, had to do with the Leonora; even I! Her voice thrilled them; ah, but it was I who taught her her notes! They praised her diamonds; yes, but once I gave her that she wanted more than diamonds, bread, and lodging and love. Beautiful they called her; she was beautiful too, when I carried her in my arms through Vienna. I am an old man now, and good for very little; and there have been days, God forgive me! when I have been angry with her; but it was not to-night. To see her there, so beautiful and so great; and to feel that after all I had a hand in it, that I invented her. Yes, yes! I had my victory to-night too; though it was so private; a secret between you and me, Monsieur? Is it not?'

I assured him of my discretion, but he hardly seemed to hear. His sad eyes had wandered away to the live coals, and he considered them pensively, as though he found them full of charming memories. I sat back, respecting his remoteness; but my silence was replete with surprised conjecture, and indeed the quaint figure of the old musician, every line of his garments redolent of ill success, had become to me, of a sudden, strangely romantic. Destiny, so amorous of surprises, of pathetic or cynical contrasts, had in this instance excelled herself. My obscure acquaintance, Maurice Cristich! The renowned Romanoff! Her name and acknowledged genius had been often in men's mouths of late, a certain luminous, scarcely sacred, glamour attaching to it, in an hundred idle stories, due perhaps as much to the wonder of her sorrowful beauty, as to any justification in knowledge, of her boundless extravagance, her magnificent fantasies, her various perversity, rumour pointing specially at those priceless diamonds, the favours not altogether gratuitous it was said of exalted personages. And with all deductions made, for malice, for the ingenuity of the curious, the impression of her perversity was left; she remained enigmatical and notorious, a somewhat scandalous heroine! And Cristich had known her; he had, as he declared, and his accent was not that of bragadoccio, invented her. The conjuncture puzzled and fascinated me. It did not make Cristich less interesting, nor the prima-donna more perspicuous.

By-and-by the violinist looked up at me; he smiled with a little dazed air, as though his thoughts had been a far journey.

'Pardon me, Monsieur! I beg you to fill your glass. I seem a poor host; but to tell you the truth, I was dreaming; I was quite away, quite away.'

He threw out his hands, with a vague expansive gesture.

'Dear child!' he said to the flames, in French; 'good little one! I do not forget thee.' And he began to tell me.

'It was when I was at Vienna, ah! a long while ago. I was not rich but neither was I very poor; I still had my little patrimony, and I lived in the — Strasse, very economically; it is a quarter which many artists frequent. I husbanded my resources, that I might be able to work away at my art without the tedium of making it a means of livelihood. I refused many offers to play in public, that I might have more leisure. I should not do that now; but then, I was very confident; I had great faith in me. And I worked very hard at my symphony, and I was full of desire to write an opera. It was a tall dark house, where I lived; there were many other lodgers, but I knew scarcely any of them. I went about with my head full of music and I had my violin; I had no time to seek acquaintance. Only my neighbour, at the other side of my passage, I knew slightly and bowed to him when we met on the stairs. He was a dark, lean man, of a very distinguished air; he must have lived very hard, he had death in his face. He was not an artist, like the rest of us: I suspect he was a great profligate, and a gambler; but he had the manners of a gentleman. And when I came to talk to him, he displayed the greatest knowledge of music that I have ever known. And it was the same with all; he talked divinely, of everything in the world, but very wildly and bitterly. He seemed to have been everywhere, and done everything; and at last to be tired of it all; and of himself the most. From the people of the house I heard that he was a Pole; noble, and very poor; and, what surprised me, that he had a daughter with him, a little girl. I used to pity this child, who must have lived quite alone. For the Count was always out, and the child never appeared with him; and, for the rest, with his black spleen and tempers, he must have been but sorry company for a little girl. I wished much to see her; for you see, Monsieur! I am fond of children, almost as much as of music; and one day it came about. I was at home with my violin; I had been playing all the evening some songs I had made; and once or twice I had seemed to be interrupted by little, tedious sounds. At last I stopped, and opened the door; and there, crouching down, I found the most beautiful little creature I had ever seen in my life. It was the child of my neighbour. Yes, Monsieur! you divine, you divine! That was the Leonora!'

'And she is not your compatriot?' I asked.

'A Hungarian? ah, no! yet every piece of her pure Slav. But I weary you, Monsieur; I make a long story.'

I protested my interest; and after a little side glance of dubious scrutiny, he continued in a constrained monotone, as one who told over to himself some rosary of sad enchanting memories.

'Ah, yes! she was beautiful; that mysterious, sad Slavonic beauty! a thing quite special and apart. And, as a child, it was more tragical and strange; that dusky hair! those profound and luminous eyes! seeming to mourn over tragedies they have never known. A strange, wild, silent child! She might have been eight or nine, then; but her little soul was hungry for music. It was a veritable passion; and when she became at last my good friend, she told me how often she had lain for long hours outside my door, listening to my violin. I gave her a kind of scolding, such as one could to so beautiful a little creature, for the passage was draughty and cold, and sent her away with some *bon-bons*. She shook back her long, dark hair: 'You are not angry, and I am not naughty,' she said: 'and I shall come back. I thank you for your *bon-bons;* but I like your music better than *bon-bons*, or fairy tales, or anything in the world.'

'But she never came back to the passage again, Monsieur! The next time I came across the Count, I sent her an invitation, a little diffidently, for he had never spoken to me of her, and he was a strange and difficult man. Now, he simply shrugged his shoulders, with a smile, in which, for once, there seemed more entertainment than malice. The child could visit me when she chose; if it amused either of us, so much the better. And we were content, and she came to me often; after a while, indeed, she was with me almost always. Child as she was, she had already the promise of her magnificent voice; and I taught her to use it, to sing, and to play on the piano and on the violin, to which she took the most readily. She was like a singing bird in the room, such pure, clear notes! And she grew very fond of me; she would fall asleep at last in my arms, and so stay until the Count would take her with him when he entered, long after midnight. He came to me naturally for her soon; and they never seemed long those hours that I watched over her sleep. I never knew him harsh or unkind to the child; he seemed simply indifferent to her as to everything else. He had exhausted life and he hated it; and he knew that death was on him, and he hated that even more. And yet he was careful of her after a fashion, buying her *bon-bons* and little costumes, when he was in the vein, pitching his voice softly when he would stay and talk to me, as though he relished her sleep. One night he did not come to fetch her at all, I had wrapped a blanket round the child where she lay on my bed, and had sat down to watch by her and presently I too fell asleep. I do not know how long I slept but when I woke there was a gray light in the room, I was very cold and stiff, but I could hear close by, the soft, regular breathing of the child. There was a great uneasiness on me, and after a while I stole out across the passage and knocked at the Count's door, there was no answer but it gave when I tried it, and so I went in. The lamp had smouldered out, there was a sick odour of *pétrol* everywhere, and the shutters were closed: but through the chinks the merciless gray dawn streamed in and showed me the Count sitting very still by the table. His face wore a most curious smile, and had not his great cavernous eyes been open, I should have believed him asleep: suddenly it came to me that he was dead. He was not a good man, monsieur, nor an amiable, but a true *virtuoso* and full of information, and I grieved. I have had Masses said for the repose of his soul.'

He paid a tribute of silence to the dead man's memory, and then he went on.

'It seemed quite natural that I should take his child. There was no one to care, no one to object; it happened quite easily. We went, the little one and I, to another part of the city. We made quite a new life. Oh! my God! it is a very long time ago.'

Quite suddenly his voice went tremulous; but after a pause, hardly perceptible, he recovered himself and continued with an accent of apology.

'I am a foolish old man, and very garrulous. It is not good to think of that, nor to talk of it; I do not know why I do. But what would you have? She loved me then, and she had the voice and the disposition of an angel. I have never been very happy. I think sometimes, monsieur, that we others, who care much for art, are not permitted that. But certainly those few, rapid days, when she was a child, were good; and yet they were the days of my defeat. I found myself out then. I was never to be a great artist, a *maestro*: a second-rate man, a good music-teacher for young ladies, a capable performer in an orchestra, what you will, but a great artist, never! Yet in those days, even when my opera failed, I had consolation, I could say, I have a child! I would have kept her with me always but it could not be, from the very first she would be a singer. I knew always that a day would come when she would not need me, she was meant to be the world's delight, and I had no right to keep her, even if I could. I held my beautiful, strange bird in her cage, until she beat her wings against the bars, then I opened the door. At the last, I think, that is all we can do for our children, our best beloved, our very heart-strings, stand free of them, let them go. The world is very weary, but we must all find that out for ourselves, perhaps when they are tired they will come home, perhaps not, perhaps not. It was to the Conservatoire, at Milan, that I sent her finally, and it was at La Scala that she afterwards appeared, and at La Scala too, poor child, she met her evil genius, the man named Romanoff, a baritone in her company, own son of the devil, whom she married. Ah, if I could have prevented it, if I could have prevented it!'

He lapsed into a long silence; a great weariness seemed to have come over him, and in the gray light which filtered in through the dingy window blinds, his face was pinched and wasted, unutterably old and forlorn.

'But I did not prevent it,' he said at last, 'for all my good will, perhaps merely hastened it by unseasonable interference. And so we went in different ways, with anger I fear, and at least with sore hearts and misunderstanding.'

He spoke with an accent of finality, and so sadly that in a sudden rush of pity I was moved to protest.

'But, surely you meet sometimes; surely this woman, who was as your own child –'

He stopped me with a solemn, appealing gesture.

'You are young, and you do not altogether understand. You must not judge her; you must not believe, that she forgets, that she does not care. Only, it is better like this, because it could never be as before. I could not help her. I want nothing that she can give me, no not anything; I have my memories! I hear of her, from time to time; I hear what the world says of her, the imbecile world, and I smile. Do I not know best? I, who carried her in my arms, when she was that high!'

And in effect the old violinist smiled, it was as though he had surprised my secret of dissatisfaction, and found it, like the malice of the world, too ignorant to resent. The edge of his old, passionate adoration had remained bright and keen through the years; and it imparted a strange brilliancy to his eyes, which half convinced me, as presently, with a resumption of his usual air of diffident courtesy, he ushered me out into the vague, spring dawn. And yet, when I had parted from him and was making my way somewhat wearily to my own quarters, my first dubious impression remained. My imagination was busy with the story I had heard, striving quite vainly to supply omissions, to fill in meagre outlines Yes! quite vainly! the figure of the Romanoff was left, ambiguous and unexplained; hardly acquitted in my mind of a certain callousness, an ingratitude almost vulgar as it started out from time to time, in contraposition against that forlorn old age.

III

I saw him once more at the little restaurant in Soho, before a sudden change of fortune, calling me abroad for an absence, as it happened, of years, closed the habit of our society. He gave me the god-speed of a brother artist, though mine was not the way of music, with many prophesies of my success; and the pressure of his hand, as he took leave of me, was tremulous.

'I am an old man, monsieur, and we may not meet again, in this world. I wish you all the chances you deserve in Paris; but I – I shall greatly miss you. If you come back in time, you will find me in the old places; and if not – there are things of mine, which I should wish you to have, that shall be sent you.'

And indeed it proved to be our last meeting. I went to Paris; a fitful correspondence intervened, grew infrequent, ceased; then a little later, came to me the notification, very brief and official, of his death in the French Hospital of pneumonia. It was followed by a few remembrances of him, sent at his request, I learnt, by the priest who had administered to him the last offices: some books that he had greatly cherished, works of Glück, for the most part; an antique ivory crucifix of very curious workmanship; and his violin, a beautiful instrument dated 1670 and made at Nuremberg, yet with a tone which seemed to me, at least, as fine as that of the Cremonas. It had an intrinsic value to me, apart from its associations; for I too was something of an amateur, and since this seasoned melodious wood had come into my possession, I was inspired to take my facility more seriously. To play in public, indeed, I had neither leisure nor desire: but in certain *salons* of my acquaintance, where music was much in vogue, I made from time to time a desultory appearance. I set down these facts, because as it happened, this ineffectual talent of mine, which poor Cristich's legacy had recalled to life, was to procure me an interesting encounter. I remember the occasion well, it was too appropriate to be forgotten – as though my old friend's lifeless fiddle, which had yet survived so many *maestri*, was to be a direct instrument of the completion of his story, the resurrection of those dormant and unsatisfied curiosities which still now and again concerned me. I had played at an house where I was a stranger; brought there by a friend, to whose insistence I had yielded somewhat reluctantly; although he had assured me, and, I believe, with reason, that it was a house where the indirect, or Attic invitation greatly prevailed, in brief, a place where one met very queer people. The hostess was American, a charming woman, of unimpeachable antecedents; but her passion for society, which, while it should always be interesting, was not always equally reputable, had exposed her evenings to the suspicion of her compatriots. And when I had discharged my part in the programme and had leisure to look around me, I saw at a glance that their suspicion was justified; very queer people indeed were there. The large hot rooms were cosmopolitan: infidels and Jews, everybody and nobody; a scandalously promiscuous assemblage! And there, with a half start, which was not at first recognition, my eyes stopped before a face which brought to me a confused rush of memories. It was that of a woman who sat on an ottoman in the smallest room which was almost empty. Her companion was a small, vivacious man with a gray imperial, and the red ribbon in his buttonhole, to whose continuous stream of talk, eked out with meridional gestures, she had the air of being listlessly resigned. Her dress, a marvel of discretion, its colour the yellow of old ivory, was of some very rich and stiff stuff cut square to her neck; that, and her great black hair, clustered to a crimson rose at the top of her head, made the pallor of her face a thing to marvel at. Her beauty was at once sombre and illuminating, and youthful no less. The woman of thirty: but her complexion, and her arms, which were bare, were soft in texture as a young girl's.

I made my way as well as I could for the crowd, to my hostess, listened, with what patience I might, to some polite praise of my playing, and made my request.

'Mrs Destrier, I have an immense favour to ask; introduce me to Madame Romanoff!'

She gave me a quick, shrewd smile; then I remembered stories of her intimate quaintness.

'My dear young man! I have no objection. Only I warn you, she is not conversational; you will make no good of it, and you will be disappointed; perhaps that will be best. Please remember, I am responsible for nobody.'

'Is she so dangerous?' I asked. 'But never mind; I believe that I have something to say which may interest her.'

'Oh, for that!' she smiled elliptically; 'yes, she is most dangerous. But I will introduce you; you shall tell me how you succeed.'

I bowed and smiled; she laid a light hand on my arm; and I piloted her to the desired corner. It seemed that the chance was with me. The little fluent Provençal had just vacated his seat; and when the prima-donna had acknowledged the hasty mention of my name, with a bare inclination of her head, I was emboldened to succeed to it. And then I was silent. In the perfection of that dolorous face, I could not but be reminded of the tradition which has always ascribed something fatal and inevitable to the possession of great gifts: of genius or uncommon fortune, or singular personal beauty; and the common-place of conversation failed me.

After a while she looked askance at me, with a sudden flash of resentment.

'You speak no French, Monsieur! And yet you write it well enough; I have read your stories.'

46

I acknowledged Madame's irony, permitted myself to hope that my efforts had met with Madame's approval.

'*A la bonne heure!* I perceive you also speak it. Is that why you wished to be presented, to hear my criticisms?'

'Let me answer that question when you have answered mine.'

She glanced curiously over her feathered fan, then with the slightest upward inclination of her statuesque shoulders – 'I admire your books; but are your women quite just? I prefer your playing.'

'That is better, Madame! It was to talk of that I came.'

'Your playing?'

'My violin.'

'You want me to look at it? It is a Cremona?'

'It is not a Cremona; but if you like, I will give it you.'

Her dark eyes shone out in amazed amusement.

'You are eccentric, Monsieur! but your nation has a privilege of eccentricity. At least, you amuse me; and I have wearied myself enough this long evening. Show me your violin; I am something of a *virtuosa*.'

I took the instrument from its case, handed it to her in silence, watching her gravely. She received it with the dexterous hands of a musician, looked at the splendid stains on the back, then bent over towards the light in a curious scrutiny of the little, faded signature of its maker, the *fecit* of an obscure Bavarian of the seventeenth century; and it was a long time before she raised her eyes.

When she spoke, her rich voice had a note of imperious entreaty in it. 'Your violin interests me, Monsieur! Oh, I know that wood! It came to you – ?'

'A legacy from an esteemed friend.'

She shot back. 'His name?' with the flash which I waited for.

'Maurice Cristich, Madame!'

We were deserted in our corner. The company had strayed in, one by one, to the large *salon* with the great piano, where a young Russian musician, a pupil of Chopin, sat down to play, with no conventional essay of preliminary chords, an expected morsel. The strains of it wailed in just then, through the heavy, screening curtains; a mad *valse* of his own, that no human feet could dance to, a pitiful, passionate thing that thrilled the nerves painfully, ringing the changes between voluptuous sorrow and the merriment of devils, and burdened always with the weariness of 'all the Russias,' the proper *Welt-schmerz* of a young, disconsolate people. It seemed to charge the air, like electricity, with passionate undertones; it gave intimate facilities, and a tense personal note to our interview.

'A legacy! so he is gone.' She swayed to me with a wail in her voice, in a sort of childish abandonment: 'and *you* tell me! Ah!' she drew back, chilling suddenly with a touch of visible suspicion. 'You hurt me, Monsieur! Is it a stroke at random? You spoke of a gift; you say you knew, esteemed him. You were with him? Perhaps, a message . . . ?'

'He died alone, Madame! I have no message. If there were none, it might be, perhaps, that he believed you had not cared for it. If that were wrong, I could tell you that you were not forgotten. Oh! he loved you! I had his word for it, and the story. The violin is yours – do not mistake me; it is not for your sake but his. He died alone; value it, as I should, Madame!'

They were insolent words, perhaps cruel, provoked from me by the mixed nature of my attraction to her; the need of turning a reasonable and cool front to that pathetic beauty, that artful music, which whipped jaded nerves to mutiny. The arrow in them struck so true, that I was shocked at my work. It transfixed the child in her, latent in most women, which moaned at my feet; so that for sheer shame as though it were actually a child I had hurt, I could have fallen and kissed her hands.

'Oh, you judge me hard, you believe the worst of me and why not? I am against the world! At least he might have taught you to be generous, that kind old man! Have I forgotten do you think? Am I so happy then? Oh it is a just question, the world busies itself with me, and you are in the lap of its tongues. Has it ever accused me of that, of happiness? Cruel, cruel! I have paid my penalties, and a woman is not free to do as she will, but would not I have gone to him, for a word, a sign? Yes, for the sake of my childhood. And to-night when you showed me that,' her white hand swept over the violin with something of a caress, 'I thought it had come, yes, from the grave, and you make it more bitter by readings of your own. You strike me hard.'

I bent forward in real humility, her voice had tears in it, though her splendid eyes were hard.

'Forgive me, Madame! a vulgar stroke at random. I had no right to make it, he told me only good of you. Forgive me, and for proof of your pardon – I am serious now – take his violin.'

Her smile, as she refused me, was full of sad dignity.

'You have made it impossible, Monsieur! It would remind me only now of how ill you think of me. I beg you to keep it.'

The music had died away suddenly, and its ceasing had been followed by a loud murmur of applause. The prima-donna rose, and stood for a moment observing me, irresolutely.

'I leave you and your violin, Monsieur! I have to sing presently, with such voice as our talk has left me. I bid you both adieu!'

'Ah, Madame!' I deprecated, 'you will think again of this, I will send it you in the morning. I have no right . . .'

She shook her head, then with a sudden flash of amusement, or fantasy – 'I agree, Monsieur! on a condition. To prove your penitence you shall bring it to me yourself.'

I professed that her favour overpowered me. She named an hour when she would be at home: an address in the Avenue des Champs Elysées, which I noted on my tablets.

'Not adieu, then Monsieur! but *au revoir.*'

I bowed perplexedly, holding the curtain aside to let her sweep through; and once more she turned back, gathering up her voluminous train, to repeat with a glance and accent, which I found mystifying: 'Remember, Monsieur! It is only *au revoir.*'

That last glimpse of her, with the strange mockery and an almost elfish malice in her fine eyes, went home with me later to cause vague disquiet and fresh suspicion of her truth. The spell of her extraordinary, personal charm removed, doubt would assert itself. Was she quite sincere? Was her fascination not a questionable one? Might not that almost childish outburst of a grief so touching, and at the time convincing, be after all factitious; the movement of a born actress and enchauntress of men, quick to seize as by a nice professional instinct the opportunity of an effect? Had her whole attitude been a deliberate pose, a sort of trick? The sudden changes in her subtle voice, the under current of mockery in an invitation which seemed inconsequent, put me on my guard, reinforced all my deep-seated prejudices against the candour of the feminine soul. It left me with a vision of her, fantastically vivid, raccounting to an intimate circle, to an accompaniment of some discreet laughter and the popping of champagne corks, the success of her imposition, the sentimental concessions which she had extorted from a notorious student of cynical moods.

A dangerous woman! cried Mrs. Destrier with the world, which might conceivably be right; at least I was fain to add, a woman whose laughter would be merciless. Certainly, I had no temper for adventures; and a visit to Madame Romanoff on so sentimental an errand seemed to me, the more I pondered it, to partake of this quality to be rich in distasteful possibilities. Must I write myself pusillanimous, if I confess that I never made it, that I committed my old friend's violin into the hands of the woman who had been his pupil by the vulgar aid of a *commissionnaire*?

Pusillanimous or simply prudent; or perhaps cruelly unjust, to a person who had paid penalties and greatly needed kindness? It is a point I have never been able to decide, though I have tried to raise theories on the ground of her acquiescence. It seemed to me on the cards, that my fiddle bestowed so cavalierly, should be refused. And yet even the fact of her retaining it is open to two interpretations, and Cristich testified for her. Maurice Cristich! Madame Romanoff! the renowned Romanoff, Maurice Cristich! Have I been pusillanimous, prudent or merely cruel? For the life of me I cannot say!

SOUVENIRS OF AN EGOIST

SOUVENIRS OF AN EGOIST

Eheu fugaces! How that air carries me back, that air ground away so unmercifully, *sans* tune, *sans* time on a hopelessly discordant barrel-organ, right underneath my window. It is being bitterly execrated, I know, by the literary gentleman who lives in chambers above me, and by the convivial gentleman who has a dinner party underneath. It has certainly made it impossible for me to continue the passage in my new Fugue in A minor, which was being transferred so flowingly from my own brain on to the score when it interrupted me. But for all that, I have a shrewd suspicion that I shall bear its unmusical torture as long at it lasts, and eventually send away the frowsy foreigner, who no doubt is playing it, happy with a fairly large coin.

Yes: for the sake of old times, for the old emotion's sake – for Ninette's sake, I put up with it, not altogether sorry for the recollections it has aroused.

How vividly it brings it all back! Though I am a rich man now, and so comfortably domiciled; though the fashionable world are so eager to lionise me, and the musical world look upon me almost as a god, and to-morrow hundreds of people will be turned away, for want of space, from the Hall where I am to play, just I alone, my last Fantaisie, it was not so very many years ago that I trudged along, fiddling for half-pence in the streets. Ninette and I – Ninette with her barrel-organ, and I fiddling. Poor little Ninette – that air was one of the four her organ played. I wonder what has become of her? Dead, I should hope, poor child. Now that I am successful and famous, a Baron of the French Empire, it is not altogether unpleasant to think of the old, penniless, vagrant days, by a blazing fire in a thick carpeted room, with the November night shut outside. I am rather an epicure of my emotions, and my work is none the worse for it.

'Little egoist,' I remember Lady Greville once said of me, 'he has the true artistic susceptibility. All his sensations are so much grist for his art.'

But it is of Ninette, not Lady Greville, that I think to-night, Ninette's childish face that the dreary grinding organ brings up before me, not Lady Greville's aquiline nose and delicate artificial complexion.

Although I am such a great man now, I should find it very awkward to be obliged to answer questions as to my parentage and infancy.

Even my nationality I could not state precisely, though I know I am as much Italian as English, perhaps rather more. From Italy I have inherited my genius and enthusiasm for art, from England I think I must have got my common-sense, and the capacity of keeping the money which I make; also a certain natural coldness of disposition, which those who only know me as a public character do not dream of. All my earliest memories are very vague and indistinct. I remember tramping over France and Italy with a man and woman – they were Italian, I believe – who beat me, and a fiddle, which I loved passionately, and which I cannot remember having ever been without. They are very shadowy presences now, and the name of the man I have forgotten. The woman, I think, was called Maddalena. I am ignorant whether they were related to me in any way: I know that I hated them bitterly, and eventually, after a worse beating than usual, ran away from them. I never cared for any one except my fiddle, until I knew Ninette.

I was very hungry and miserable indeed when that rencontre came about. I wonder sometimes what would have happened if Ninette had not come to the rescue, just at that particular juncture. Would some other salvation have appeared, or would – well, well, if one once begins wondering what would have happened if certain accidents in one's life had not befallen one when they did, where will one come to a stop? Anyhow, when I had escaped from my taskmasters, a wretched, puny child of ten, undersized and shivering, clasping a cheap fiddle in my arms, lost in the huge labyrinth of Paris, without a *sou* in my rags to save me from starvation, I *did* meet Ninette, and that, after all, is the main point.

It was at the close of my first day of independence, a wretched November evening, very much like this one. I had wandered about all day, but my efforts had not been rewarded by a single coin. My fiddle was old and warped, and injured by the rain; its whining was even more repugnant to my own sensitive ear, than to that of the casual passer-by. I was in despair. How I hated all the few well-dressed, well-to-do people who were out on the Boulevards, on that inclement night. I wandered up and down hoping against hope, until I was too tired to stand, and then I crawled under the shelter of a covered passage, and flung myself down on the ground, to die, as I hoped, crying bitterly.

The alley was dark and narrow, and I did not see at first that it had another occupant. Presently a hand was put out and touched me on the shoulder.

I started up in terror, though the touch was soft and need not have alarmed me. I found it came from a little girl, for she was really about my own age, though then she seemed to me very big and protecting. But she was tall and strong for her age, and I, as I have said, was weak and undersized.

'Chut! little boy,' said Ninette; 'what are you crying for?'

And I told her my story, as clearly as I could, through my sobs; and soon a pair of small arms were thrown round my neck, and a smooth little face laid against my wet one caressingly. I felt as if half my troubles were over.

'Don't cry, little boy,' said Ninette grandly; 'I will take care of you. If you like, you shall live with me. We will make a *ménage* together. What is your profession?'

I showed her my fiddle, and the sight of its condition caused fresh tears to flow.

'Ah!' she said, with a smile of approval, 'a violinist – good! I too am an artiste. You ask my instrument? There it is!'

And she pointed to an object on the ground beside her, which I had, at first, taken to be a big box, and dimly hoped might contain eatables. My respect for my new friend suffered a little diminution. Already I felt instinctively that to play the fiddle, even though it is an old, a poor one, is to be something above a mere organ-grinder.

But I did not express this feeling – was not this little girl going to take me home with her? Would not she, doubtless, give me something to eat?

My first impulse was an artistic one; that was of Italy. The concealment of it was due to the English side of me – the practical side.

I crept close to the little girl; she drew me to her protectingly.

'What is thy name, *p'tit*?' she said.

'Anton,' I answered, for that was what the woman Maddalena had called me. Her husband, if he was her husband, never gave me any title, except when he was abusing me, and then my names were many and unmentionable. Nowadays I am the Baron Antonio Antonelli, of the Legion of Honour, but that is merely an extension of the old concise Anton, so far as I know, the only name I ever had.

'Anton?' repeated the little girl, 'that is a nice name to say. Mine is Ninette.'

We sat in silence in our sheltered nook, waiting until the rain should stop, and very soon I began to whimper again.

'I am so hungry, Ninette,' I said; 'I have eaten nothing to-day.'

In the literal sense this was a lie; I had eaten some stale crusts in the early morning, before I gave my taskmasters the slip, but the hunger was true enough.

Ninette began to reproach herself for not thinking of this before. After much fumbling in her pocket, she produced a bit of *brioche*, an apple, and some cold chestnuts.

'*V'la*, Anton,' she said, 'pop those in your mouth. When we get home we will have supper together. I have bread and milk at home. And we will buy two hot potatoes from the man on the *quai*.'

I ate the unsatisfying morsels ravenously, Ninette watching me with an approving nod the while. When they were finished, the weather was a little better, and Ninette said we might move. She slung the organ over her shoulder – it was a small organ, though heavy for a child; but she was used to it, and trudged along under its weight like a woman. With her free hand she caught hold of me and led me along the wet streets, proudly home. Ninette's home! Poor little Ninette! It was colder and barer than these rooms of mine now; it had no grand piano, and no thick carpets; and in the place of pictures and *bibelots*, its walls were only wreathed in cobwebs. Still it was drier than the streets of Paris, and if it had been a palace it could not have been more welcome to me than it was that night.

The *ménage* of Ninette was a strange one! There was a tumbledown deserted house in the Montparnasse district. It stood apart, in an overgrown weedy garden, and has long ago been pulled down. It was uninhabited; no one but a Parisian *gamine* could have lived in it, and Ninette had long occupied it, unmolested, save by the rats. Through the broken palings in the garden she had no difficulty in passing, and as its back door had fallen to pieces, there was nothing to bar her further entry. In one of the few rooms which had its window intact, right at the top of the house, a mere attic, Ninette had installed herself and her scanty goods, and henceforward this became my home also.

It has struck me since as strange that the child's presence should not have been resented by the owner. But I fancy the house had some story connected with it. It was, I believe, the property of an old and infirm miser, who in his reluctance to part with any of his money in repairs had overreached himself, and let his property become valueless. He could not let it, and he would not pull it down. It remained therefore an eyesore to the neighbourhood, until his death put it in the possession of a less avaricious successor. The proprietor never came near the place, and with the neighbours it had a bad repute, and they avoided it as much as possible. It stood, as I have said, alone, and in its own garden, and Ninette's occupation of it may have passed unnoticed, while even if any one of the poor people living around had known of her, it was, after all, nobody's business to interfere.

When I was last in Paris I went to look for the house, but all traces of it had vanished, and over the site, so far as I could fix it, a narrow street of poor houses flourished.

Ninette introduced me to her domain with a proud air of ownership. She had a little store of charcoal, with which she proceeded to light a fire in the grate, and by its fitful light prepared our common supper – bread and radishes, washed down by a pennyworth of milk, of which, I have no doubt, I received the lion's share. As a dessert we munched, with much relish, the steaming potatoes that Ninette had bought from a stall in the street, and had kept warm in the pocket of her apron.

And so, as Ninette said, we made a *ménage* together. How that old organ brings it all back. My fiddle was useless after the hard usage it received that day. Ninette and I went out on our rounds together, but for the present I was a sleeping partner in the firm, and all I could do was to grind occasionally when Ninette's arm ached, or pick up the sous that were thrown us. Ninette was, as a rule, fairly successful. Since her mother had died, a year before, leaving her the organ as her sole legacy, she had lived mainly by that instrument; although she often increased her income in the evenings, when organ-grinding was more than ever at a discount, by selling bunches of violets and other flowers as button-holes.

With her organ she had a regular beat, and a distinct *clientèle*. Children playing with their *bonnes* in the gardens of the Tuileries and the Luxembourg were her most productive patrons. Of course we had bad days as well as good, and in winter it was especially bad; but as a rule we managed fairly to make both ends meet. Sometimes we carried home as much as five francs as the result of the day's campaign, but this, of course, was unusual.

Ninette was not precisely a pretty child, but she had a very bright face, and, wonderful gray eyes. When she smiled, which was often, her face was very attractive, and a good many people were induced to throw a sou for the smile which they would have assuredly grudged to the music.

Though we were about the same age, the position which it might have been expected we should occupy was reversed. It was Ninette who petted and protected me – I who clung to her.

I was very fond of Ninette, certainly. I should have died in those days if it had not been for her, and sometimes I am surprised at the tenacity of my tenderness for her. As much as I ever cared for anything except my art, I cared for Ninette. But still she was never the first with me, as I must have been with her. I was often fretful and discontented, sometimes, I fear, ready to reproach her for not taking more pains to alleviate our misery, but all the time of our partnership Ninette never gave me a cross word. There was something maternal about her affection, which withstood all ungratefulness. She was always ready to console me when I was miserable, and throw her arms round me and kiss me when I was cold; and many a time, I am sure, when the day's earnings had been scanty, the little girl must have gone to sleep hungry, that I might not be stinted in my supper.

One of my grievances, and that the sorest of all, was the loss of my beloved fiddle. This, for all her goodwill, Ninette was powerless to allay.

'Dear Anton,' she said, 'do not mind about it. I earn enough for both with my organ, and some day we shall save enough to buy thee a new fiddle. When we are together, and have got food and charcoal, what does it matter about an old fiddle? Come, eat thy supper, Anton, and I will light the fire. Never mind, dear Anton.' And she laid her soft little cheek against mine with a pleading look.

'Don't,' I cried, pushing her away, 'you can't understand, Ninette; you can only grind an organ – just four tunes, always the same. But I loved my fiddle, loved it! loved it!' I cried passionately. 'It could talk to me, Ninette, and tell me beautiful, new things, always beautiful, and always new. Oh, Ninette, I shall die if I cannot play!'

It was always the same cry, and Ninette, if she could not understand, and was secretly a little jealous, was as distressed as I was; but what could she do?

Eventually, I got my violin, and it was Ninette who gave it me. The manner of its acquirement was in this wise.

Ninette would sometimes invest some of her savings in violets, which she divided with me, and made into nosegays for us to sell in the streets at night.

Theatre doors and frequented places on the Boulevards were our favourite spots.

One night we had taken up our station outside the Opéra, when a gentleman stopped on his way in, and asked Ninette for a button-hole. He was in evening dress and in a great hurry.

'How much?' he asked shortly.

'Ten sous, M'sieu,' said exorbitant little Ninette, expecting to get two at the most.

The gentleman drew out some coins hastily and selected a bunch from the basket.

'Here is a franc,' he said, 'I cannot wait for change,' and putting a coin into Ninette's hand he turned into the theatre.

Ninette ran towards me with her eyes gleaming; she held up the piece of money exultantly.

'Tiens, Anton!' she cried, and I saw that it was not a franc, as we had thought at first, but a gold Napoleon.

I believe the good little boy and girl in the story-books would have immediately sought out the unfortunate gentleman and bid him rectify his mistake, generally receiving, so the legend runs, a far larger bonus as a reward of their integrity. I have never been a particularly good little boy, however, and I don't think it ever struck either Ninette or myself – perhaps we were not sufficiently speculative – that any other course was open to us than to profit by the mistake. Ninette began to consider how we were to spend it.

'Think of it, Anton, a whole gold *louis*. A *louis*,' said Ninette, counting laboriously, 'is twenty francs, a franc is twenty sous, Anton; how many sous are there in a louis? More than a hundred?'

But this piece of arithmetic was beyond me; I shook my head dubiously.

'What shall we buy first, Anton?' said Ninette, with sparkling eyes.

'You shall have new things, Anton, a pair of new shoes and an hat; and I –'

But I had other things than clothes in my mind's eye; I interrupted her.

'Ninette, dear little Ninette,' I said coaxingly, 'remember the fiddle.'

Ninette's face fell, but she was a tender little thing, and she showed no hesitation.

'Certainly, Anton,' she said, but with less enthusiasm, 'we will get it to-morrow – one of the fiddles you showed me in M. Boudinot's shop on the Quai. Do you think the ten-franc one will do, or the light one for fifteen francs?'

'Oh, the light one, dear Ninette,' I said; 'it is worth more than the extra money. Besides, we shall soon earn it back now. Why if you could earn such a lot as you have with your old organ, when you only have to turn an handle, think what a lot I shall make, fiddling. For you have to be something to play the fiddle, Ninette.'

'Yes,' said the little girl, wincing; 'you are right, dear Anton. Perhaps you will get rich and go away and leave me?'

'No, Ninette,' I declared grandly, 'I will always take care of you. I have no doubt I shall get rich, because I am going to be a great musician, but I shall not leave you. I will have a big house on this Champs Elysées, and then you shall come and live with me, and be my housekeeper. And in the evenings, I will play to you and make you open your eyes, Ninette. You will like me to play, you know; we are often dull in the evenings.'

'Yes,' said Ninette meekly, 'we will buy your fiddle to-morrow, dear Anton. Let us go home now.'

Poor vanished Ninette! I must often have made the little heart sore with some of the careless things I said. Yet looking back at it now, I know that I never cared for any living person so much as I did for Ninette.

I have very few illusions left now; a childhood, such as mine, does not tend to preserve them, and time and success have not made me less cynical. Still I have never let my scepticism touch that childish presence. Lady Greville once said to me, in the presence of her nephew Felix Leominster, a musician too, like myself, that we three were curiously suited, for that we were, without exception, the three most cynical persons in the universe. Perhaps in a way she was right. Yet for all her cynicism Lady Greville I know has a bundle of old and faded letters, tied up in black ribbon in some hidden drawer, that perhaps she never reads now, but that she cannot forget or destroy. They are in a bold handwriting, that is, not, I think, that of the miserable, old debauchee, her husband, from whom she has been separated since the first year of her marriage, and their envelopes bear Indian postmarks.

And Felix, who told me the history of those letters with a smile of pity on his thin, ironical lips – Felix, whose principles are adapted to his conscience and whose conscience is bounded by the law, and in whom I believe as little as he does in me, I found out by accident not so very long ago. It was on the day of All Souls, the melancholy festival of souvenirs, celebrated once a year, under the November fogs, that I strayed into the Montparnasse Cemetery, to seek inspiration for my art. And though he did not see me, I saw Felix, the prince of railers, who believes in nothing and cares for nothing except himself, for music is not with him a passion but an *agrément*. Felix bareheaded, and without his usual smile, putting fresh flowers on the grave of a little Parisian grisette, who had been his mistress and died five years ago. I thought of Balzac's 'Messe de l'Athée' and ranked Felix's inconsistency with it, feeling at the same time how natural such a paradox is. And myself, the last of the trio, at the mercy of a street organ, I cannot forget Ninette.

Though it was not until many years had passed that I heard that little criticism, the purchase of my fiddle was destined very shortly to bring my life in contact with its author. Those were the days when a certain restraint grew up between Ninette and myself. Ninette, it must be confessed, was jealous of the fiddle. Perhaps she knew instinctively that music was with me a single and absorbing passion, from which she was excluded. She was no genius, little Ninette, and her organ was nothing more to her than the means of making a livelihood; she felt not the smallest *tendresse* for it, and could not understand why a dead and inanimate fiddle, made of mere wood and catgut, should be any more to me than that. How could she know that to me it was never a dead thing, that even when it hung hopelessly out of my reach, in the window of M. Boudinot, before ever it had given out wild, impassioned music beneath my hands, it was always a live thing to me, alive and with a human, throbbing heart, vibrating with hope and passion.

So Ninette was jealous of the fiddle, and being proud in her way, she became more and more quiet and reticent, and drew herself aloof from me, although, wrapped up as I was in the double egoism of art and boyhood, I failed to notice this. I have been sorry since that any shadow of misunderstanding should have clouded the closing days of our partnership. It is late to regret now, however. When my fiddle was added to our belongings, we took to going out separately. It was more profitable, and, besides, Ninette, I think, saw that I was growing a little ashamed of her organ. On one of these occasions, as I played before a house in the Faubourg St. Germain, the turning point of my life befell me. The house, outside which I had taken my station was a large, white one, with a balcony on the first floor. This balcony was unoccupied, but the window looking to it was open, and through the lace curtains I could distinguish the sound of voices. I began to play; at first, one of the airs that Maddalena had taught me; but before it was finished, I had glided off, as usual, into an improvisation.

When I was playing like that, I threw all my soul into my fingers, and I had neither ears nor eyes for anything around me. I did not therefore notice until I had finished playing that a lady and a young man had come out into the balcony, and were beckoning to me.

'Bravo!' cried the lady enthusiastically, but she did not throw me the reward I had expected. She turned and said something to her companion, who smiled and disappeared. I waited expectantly, thinking perhaps she had sent him for her purse. Presently the door opened, and the young man issued from it. He came to me and touched me on the shoulder.

'You are to come with me,' he said, authoritatively, speaking in French, but with an English accent. I followed him, my heart beating with excitement, through the big door, into a large, handsome hall and up a broad staircase, thinking that in all my life I had never seen such a beautiful house.

He led me into a large and luxurious *salon*, which seemed to my astonished eyes like a wonderful museum. The walls were crowded with pictures, a charming composition by Gustave Moreau was lying on the grand piano, waiting until a nook could be found for it to hang. Renaissance bronzes and the work of eighteenth century silversmiths jostled one another on brackets, and on a table lay a handsome violin-case. The pale blinds were drawn down, and there was a delicious smell of flowers diffused everywhere. A lady was lying on a sofa near the window, a handsome woman of about thirty, whose dress was a miracle of lace and flimsiness.

The young man led me towards her, and she placed two delicate, jewelled hands on my shoulders, looking me steadily in the face.

'Where did you learn to play like that, my boy?' she asked.

'I cannot remember when I could not fiddle, Madame,' I answered, and that was true.

'The boy is a born musician, Felix,' said Lady Greville. 'Look at his hands.'

And she held up mine to the young man's notice; he glanced at them carelessly.

'Yes, Miladi,' said the young man, 'they are real violin hands. What were you playing just now, my lad?'

'I don't know, sir,' I said. 'I play just what comes into my head.'

Lady Greville looked at her nephew with a glance of triumph.

'What did I tell you?' she cried. 'The boy is a genius, Felix. I shall have him educated.'

'All your geese are swans, Auntie,' said the young man in English.

Lady Greville, however, ignored this thrust.

'Will you play for me now, my dear,' she said, 'as you did before – just what comes into your head?'

I nodded, and was getting my fiddle to my chin, when she stopped me.

'Not that thing,' bestowing a glance of contempt at my instrument. 'Felix, the Stradivarius.'

The young man went to the other side of the room, and returned with the case which I had noticed. He put it in my hand, with the injunction to handle it gently. I had never heard of Cremona violins, nor of my namesake Stradivarius; but at the sight of the dark seasoned wood, reposing on its blue velvet, I could not restrain a cry of admiration.

I have that same instrument in my room now, and I would not trust it in the hands of another for a million.

I lifted the violin tenderly from its case, and ran my bow up the gamut.

I felt almost intoxicated at the mellow sounds it uttered. I could have kissed the dark wood, that looked to me stained through and through with melody.

I began to play. My improvisation was a song of triumph and delight; the music, at first rapid and joyous, became slower and more solemn, as the inspiration seized me, until at last, in spite of myself, it grew into a wild and indescribable dirge, fading away in a long wail of unutterable sadness and regret. When it was over I felt exhausted and unstrung, as though virtue had gone out from me. I had played as I had never played before. The young man had turned away, and was looking out of the window. The lady on the sofa was transfigured. The languor had altogether left her, and the tears were streaming down her face, to the great detriment of the powder and enamel which composed her complexion.

She pulled me towards her, and kissed me.

'It is beautiful, terrible!' she said; 'I have never heard such strange music in my life. You must stay with me now and have masters. If you can play like that now, without culture and education, in time, when you have been taught, you will be the greatest violinist that ever lived.'

I will say of Lady Greville that, in spite of her frivolity and affectations, she does love music at the bottom of her soul, with the absorbing passion that in my eyes would absolve a person for committing all the sins in the Decalogue. If her heart could be taken out and examined I can fancy it as a shield, divided into equal fields. Perhaps, as her friends declare, one of these might bear the device 'Modes et Confections'; but I am sure that you would see on the other, even more deeply graven, the divine word 'Music.'

She is one of the few persons whose praise of any of my compositions gives me real satisfaction; and almost alone, when everybody is running, in true goose fashion, to hear my piano recitals, she knows and tells me to stick to my true vocation – the violin.

'My dear Baron,' she said, 'why waste your time playing on an instrument which is not suited to you, when you have Stradivarius waiting at home for the magic touch?'

She was right, though it is the fashion to speak of me now as a second Rubenstein. There are two or three finer pianists than I, even here in England. But I am quite sure, yes, and you are sure, too, oh my Stradivarius, that in the whole world there is nobody who can make such music out of you as I can, no one to whom you tell such stories as you tell to me. Anyone, who knows, could see by merely looking at my hands that they are violin and not piano hands.

'Will you come and live with me, Anton?' said Lady Greville, more calmly. 'I am rich, and childless; you shall live just as if you were my child. The best masters in Europe shall teach you. Tell me where to find your parents, Anton, and I will see them to-night.'

'I have no parents,' I said, 'only Ninette. I cannot leave Ninette.'

'Shade of Musset, who is Ninette?' asked Felix, turning round from the window.

I told him.

'What is to be done?' cried Lady Greville in perplexity. 'I cannot have the girl here as well, and I will not let my Phoenix go.'

'Send her to the Soeurs de la Miséricorde,' said the young man carelessly; 'you have a nomination.'

'Have I?' said Lady Greville, with a laugh. 'I am sure I did not know it. It is an excellent idea; but do you think he will come without the other? I suppose they were like brother and sister?'

'Look at him now,' said Felix, pointing to where I stood caressing the precious wood; 'he would sell his soul for that fiddle.'

Lady Greville took the hint. 'Here, Anton,' said she, 'I cannot have Ninette here – you understand, once and for all. But I will see that she is sent to a kind home, where she will want for nothing and be trained up as a servant. You need not bother about her. You will live with me and be taught, and some day, if you are good and behave, you shall go and see Ninette.'

I was irresolute, but I only said doggedly, feeling what would be the end, 'I do not want to come, if Ninette may not.'

Then Lady Greville played her trump card.

'Look, Anton,' she said, 'you see that violin. I have no need, I see, to tell you its value. If you will come with me and make no scene, you shall have it for your very own. Ninette will be perfectly happy. Do you agree?'

I looked at my old fiddle, lying on the floor. How yellow and trashy it looked beside the grand old Cremona, bedded in its blue velvet.

'I will do what you like, Madame,' I said.

'Human nature is pretty much the same in geniuses and dullards,' said Felix. 'I congratulate you, Auntie.'

And so the bargain was struck, and the new life entered upon that very day. Lady Greville sought out Ninette at once, though I was not allowed to accompany her.

I never saw Ninette again. She made no opposition to Lady Greville's scheme. She let herself be taken to the Orphanage, and she never asked, so they said, to see me again.

'She's a stupid little thing,' said Lady Greville to her nephew, on her return, 'and as plain as possible; but I suppose she was kind to the boy. They will forget each other now I hope. It is not as if they were related.'

'In that case they would already be hating each other. However, I am quite sure your protégé will forget soon enough; and, after all, you have nothing to do with the girl.'

I suppose I did not think very much of Ninette then; but what would you have? It was such a change from the old vagrant days, that there is a good deal to excuse me. I was absorbed too in the new and wonderful symmetry which music began to assume, as taught me by the master Lady Greville procured for me. When the news was broken to me, with great gentleness, that my little companion had run away from the sisters with whom she had been placed – run away, and left no traces behind her, I hardly realised how completely she would have passed away from me. I thought of her for a little while with some regret; then I remembered Stradivarius, and I could not be sorry long. So by degrees I ceased to think of her.

I lived on in Lady Greville's house, going with her, wherever she stayed – London, Paris, and Nice – until I was thirteen. Then she sent me away to study music at a small German capital, in the house of one of the few surviving pupils of Weber. We parted as we had lived together, without affection.

Personally Lady Greville did not like me; if anything, she felt an actual repugnance towards me. All the care she lavished on me was for the sake of my talent, not for myself. She took a great deal of trouble in superintending, not only my musical education, but my general culture. She designed little mediæval costumes for me, and was indefatigable in her endeavours to impart to my manners that finish which a gutter education had denied me.

There is a charming portrait of me, by a well-known English artist, that hangs now in her ladyship's drawing-room. A pale boy of twelve, clad in an old-fashioned suit of ruby velvet; a boy with huge, black eyes, and long curls of the same colour, is standing by an oak music-stand, holding before him a Cremona violin, whose rich colouring is relieved admirably by the beautiful old point lace with which the boy's doublet is slashed. It is a charming picture. The famous artist who painted it considers it his best portrait, and Lady Greville is proud of it.

But her pride is of the same quality as that which made her value my presence. I was in her eyes merely the complement of her famous fiddle.

I heard her one day express a certain feeling of relief at my approaching departure.

'You regret having taken him up?' asked her nephew curiously.

'No,' she said, 'that would be folly. He repays all one's trouble, as soon as he touches his fiddle – but I don't like him.'

'He can play like the great Pan,' says Felix,

'Yes, and like Pan he is half a beast.'

'You may make a musician out of him,' answered the young man, examining his pink nails with a certain admiration, 'but you will never make him a gentleman.'

'Perhaps not,' said Lady Greville carelessly, 'Still, Felix, he is very refined.'

Dame! I think he would own himself mistaken now. Mr. Felix Leominster himself is not a greater social success than the Baron Antonio Antonelli, of the Legion of Honour. I am as sensitive as anyone to the smallest spot on my linen, and Duchesses rave about my charming manners.

For the rest my souvenirs are not very numerous. I lived in Germany until I made my *début*, and I never heard anything more of Ninette.

The history of my life is very much the history of my art: and that you know. I have always been an art-concentrated man – self-concentrated, my friend Felix Leominster tells me frankly – and since I was a boy nothing has ever troubled the serene repose of my egoism.

It is strange considering the way people rant about the 'passionate sympathy' of my playing, the 'enormous potentiality of suffering' revealed in my music, how singularly free from passion and disturbance my life has been.

I have never let myself be troubled by what is commonly called 'love.' To be frank with you, I do not much believe in it. Of the two principal elements of which it is composed, vanity and egoism, I have too little of the former, too much of the latter, too much coldness withal in my character to suffer from it. My life has been notoriously irreproachable. I figure in polemical literature as an instance of a man who has lived in contact with the demoralizing influence of the stage, and will yet go to Heaven. *A la bonne heure!*

I am coming to the end of my souvenirs and of my cigar at the same time. I must convey a coin somehow to that dreary person outside, who is grinding now half-way down the street.

On consideration, I decide emphatically against opening the window and presenting it that way. If the fog once gets in, it will utterly spoil me for any work this evening. I feel myself in travail also of two charming little *Lieder* that all this thinking about Ninette has suggested. How would 'Chansons de Gamine' do for a title? I think it best, on second thoughts, to ring for Giacomo, my man, and send him out with the half-crown I propose to sacrifice on the altar of sentiment. Doubtless the musician is a country-woman of his, and if he pockets the coin, that is his look out.

Now if I was writing a romance, what a chance I have got. I should tell you how my organ-grinder turned out to be no other than Ninette. Of course she would not be spoilt or changed by the years – just the same Ninette. Then what scope for a pathetic scene of reconciliation and forgiveness – the whole to conclude with a peal of marriage bells, two people living together 'happy ever after.' But I am not writing a romance, and I am a musician, not a poet.

Sometimes, however, it strikes me that I should like to see Ninette again, and I find myself seeking traces of her in childish faces in the street.

The absurdity of such an expectation strikes me very forcibly afterwards, when I look at my reflection in the glass, and tell myself that I must be careful in the disposition of my parting.

Ninette, too, was my contemporary. Still I cannot conceive of her as a woman. To me she is always a child. Ninette grown up, with a draggled dress and squalling babies, is an incongruous thing that shocks my sense of artistic fitness. My fiddle is my only mistress, and while I can summon its consolation at command, I may not be troubled by the pettiness of a merely human love. But once when I was down with Roman fever, and tossed on a hotel bed, all the long, hot night, while Giacomo drowsed in a corner over 'Il Diavolo Rosa,' I seemed to miss

Ninette.

Remembering that time, I sometimes fancy that when the inevitable hour strikes, and this hand is too weak to raise the soul of melody out of Stradivarius – when, my brief dream of life and music over, I go down into the dark land, where there is no more music, and no Ninette, into the sleep from which there comes no awakening, I should like to see her again, not the woman but the child. I should like to look into the wonderful eyes of the old Ninette, to feel the soft cheek laid against mine, to hold the little brown hands, as in the old *gamin* days.

It is a foolish thought, because I am not forty yet, and with the moderate life I lead I may live to play Stradivarius for another thirty years.

There is always the hope, too, that it, when it comes, may seize me suddenly. To see it coming, that is the horrible part. I should like to be struck by lightning, with you in my arms, Stradivarius, oh, my beloved – to die playing.

The literary gentleman over my head is stamping viciously about his room. What would his language be if he knew how I have rewarded his tormentress – he whose principles are so strict that he would bear the agony for hours, sooner than give a barrel-organ sixpence to go to another street. He would be capable of giving Giacomo a sovereign to pocket my coin, if he only knew. Yet I owe that unmusical old organ a charming evening, tinged with a faint *soupçon* of melancholy which is necessary to and enhances the highest pleasure. Over the memories it has excited I have smoked a pleasant cigar – peace to its ashes!

THE STATUTE OF LIMITATIONS

THE STATUTE OF LIMITATIONS

During five years of an almost daily association with Michael Garth, in a solitude of Chili, which threw us, men of common speech, though scarcely of common interests, largely on each other's tolerance, I had grown, if not into an intimacy with him, at least into a certain familiarity, through which the salient features of his history, his character reached me. It was a singular character, and an history rich in instruction. So much I gathered from hints, which he let drop long before I had heard the end of it. Unsympathetic as the man was to me, it was impossible not to be interested by it. As our acquaintance advanced, it took (his character I mean) more and more the aspect of a difficult problem in psychology, that I was passionately interested in solving: to study it was my recreation, after watching the fluctuating course of nitrates. So that when I had achieved fortune, and might have started home immediately, my interest induced me to wait more than three months, and return in the same ship with him. It was through this delay that I am enabled to transcribe the issue of my impressions: I found them edifying, if only for their singular irony.

From his own mouth indeed I gleaned but little; although during our voyage home, in those long nights when we paced the deck together under the Southern Cross, his reticence occasionally gave way, and I obtained glimpses of a more intimate knowledge of him than the whole of our juxtaposition on the station had ever afforded me. I guessed more, however, than he told me; and what was lacking I pieced together later, from the talk of the girl to whom I broke the news of his death. He named her to me, for the first time, a day or two before that happened: a piece of confidence so unprecedented, that I must have been blind, indeed, not to have foreseen what it prefaced. I had seen her face the first time I entered his house, where her photograph hung on a conspicuous wall: the charming, oval face of a young girl, little more than a child, with great eyes, that one guessed, one knew not why, to be the colour of violets, looking out with singular wistfulness from a waving cloud of dark hair. Afterwards, he told me that it was the picture of his *fiancée*: but, before that, signs had not been wanting by which I had read a woman in his life.

Iquique is not Paris; it is not even Valparaiso; but it is a city of civilization; and but two days' ride from the pestilential stew, where we nursed our lives doggedly on quinine and hope, the ultimate hope of evasion. The lives of most Englishmen yonder, who superintended works in the interior, are held on the same tenure: you know them by a certain savage, hungry look in their eyes. In the meantime, while they wait for their luck, most of them are glad enough when business calls them down for a day or two to Iquique. There are shops and streets, lit streets through which blackeyed Senoritas pass in their lace mantilas; there are *cafés* too; and faro for those who reck of it; and bull fights, and newspapers younger than six weeks; and in the harbour, taking in their fill of nitrates, many ships, not to be considered without envy, because they are coming, within a limit of days to England. But Iquique had no charm for Michael Garth, and when one of us must go, it was usually I, his subordinate, who being delegated, congratulated myself on his indifference. Hard-earned dollars melted at Iquique; and to Garth, life in Chili had long been solely a matter of amassing them. So he stayed on, in the prickly heat of Agnas Blancas, and grimly counted the days, and the money (although his nature, I believe, was fundamentally generous, in his set concentration of purpose, he had grown morbidly avaricious) which should restore him to his beautiful mistress. Morose, reti-

cent, unsociable as he had become, he had still, I discovered by degrees, a leaning towards the humanities, a nice taste, such as could
only be the result of much knowledge, in the fine things of literature.
His infinitesimal library, a few French novels, an Horace, and some
well thumbed volumes of the modern English poets in the familiar
edition of Tauchnitz, he put at my disposal, in return for a collection,
somewhat similar, although a little larger, of my own. In his rare moments of amiability, he could talk on such matters with *verve* and origi-
nality: more usually he preferred to pursue with the bitterest animos-
ity an abstract fetish which he called his 'luck'. He was by temperament an enraged pessimist; and I could believe, that he seriously at-
tributed to Providence, some quality inconceivably malignant, directed
in all things personally against himself. His immense bitterness and
his careful avarice, alike, I could explain, and in a measure justify, when
I came to understand that he had felt the sharpest stings of poverty,
and, moreover, was passionately in love, in love *comme on ne l'est plus*.
As to what his previous resources had been, I knew nothing, nor why
they had failed him; but I gathered that the crisis had come, just when
his life was complicated by the sudden blossoming of an old friendship into love, in his case, at least, to be complete and final. The girl too
was poor; they were poorer than most poor persons: how could he
refuse the post, which, through the good offices of a friend, was just
then unexpectedly offered him? Certainly, it was abroad; it implied
five years' solitude in Equatorial America. Separation and change were
to be accounted; perhaps, disease and death, and certainly his 'luck',
which seemed to include all these. But it also promised, when the term
of his exile was up, and there were means of shortening it, a certain
competence, and very likely wealth; escaping those other contingen-
cies, marriage. There seemed no other way. The girl was very young:
there was no question of an early marriage; there was not even a definite engagement. Garth would take no promise from her: only for himself, he was her bound lover while he breathed; would keep himself
free to claim her, when he came back in five years, or ten, or twenty, if
she had not chosen better. He would not bind her; but I can imagine

how impressive his dark, bitter face must have made this renunciation to the little girl with the violet eyes; how tenderly she repudiated her freedom. She went out as a governess, and sat down to wait. And absence only rivetted faster the chain of her affection: it set Garth more securely on the pedestal of her idea; for in love it is most usually the reverse of that social maxim, *les absents ont toujours tort*, which is true.

Garth, on his side, writing to her, month by month, while her picture smiled on him from the wall, if he was careful always to insist on her perfect freedom, added, in effect, so much more than this, that the renunciation lost its benefit. He lived in a dream of her; and the memory of her eyes and her hair was a perpetual presence with him, less ghostly than the real company among whom he mechanically transacted his daily business. Burnt away and consumed by desire of her living arms, he was counting the hours which still prevented him from them. Yet, when his five years were done, he delayed his return, although his economies had justified it; settled down for another term of five years, which was to be prolonged to seven. Actually, the memory of his old poverty, with its attendant dishonours, was grown a fury, pursuing him ceaselessly with whips. The lust of gain, always for the girl's sake, and so, as it were, sanctified, had become a second nature to him; an intimate madness, which left him no peace. His worst nightmare was to wake with a sudden shock, imagining that he had lost everything, that he was reduced to his former poverty: a cold sweat would break all over him before he had mastered the horror. The recurrence of it, time after time, made him vow grimly, that he would go home a rich man, rich enough to laugh at the fantasies of his luck. Latterly, indeed, this seemed to have changed; so that his vow was fortunately kept. He made money lavishly at last: all his operations were successful, even those which seemed the wildest gambling: and the most forlorn speculations turned round, and shewed a pretty harvest, when Garth meddled with their stock.

And all the time he was waiting there, and scheming, at Agnas Blancas, in a feverish concentration of himself upon his ultimate reunion with the girl at home, the man was growing old: gradually at first, and insensibly; but towards the end, by leaps and starts, with an increasing consciousness of how he aged and altered, which did but feed his black melancholy. It was borne upon him, perhaps, a little brutally, and not by direct self-examination, when there came another photograph from England. A beautiful face still but certainly the face of a woman, who had passed from the grace of girlhood (seven years now separated her from it), to a dignity touched with sadness: a face, upon which life had already written some of its cruelties. For many days after this arrival, Garth was silent and moody, even beyond his wont: then he studiously concealed it. He threw himself again furiously into his economic battle; he had gone back to the inspiration of that other, older portrait: the charming, oval face of a young girl, almost a child, with great eyes, that one guessed, one knew not why, to be the colour of violets.

As the time of our departure approached, a week or two before we had gone down to Valparaiso, where Garth had business to wind up, I was enabled to study more intimately the morbid demon which possessed him. It was the most singular thing in the world: no man had hated the country more, had been more passionately determined for a period of years to escape from it; and now that his chance was come the emotion with which he viewed it was nearer akin to terror than to the joy of a reasonable man who is about to compass the desire of his life. He had kept the covenant which he had made with himself; he was a rich man, richer than he had ever meant to be. Even now he was full of vigour, and not much past the threshold of middle age, and he was going home to the woman whom for the best part of fifteen years he had adored with an unexampled constancy, whose fidelity had been to him all through that exile as the shadow of a rock in a desert land: he was going home to an honourable marriage. But withal he was a man with an incurable sadness; miserable and afraid. It seemed to me at times that he would have been glad if she had kept her troth less well, had only availed herself of that freedom which he gave her, to disregard her promise. And this was the more strange in that I never doubted the strength of his attachment; it remained engrossing and unchanged, the largest part of his life. No alien shadow had ever come between him and the memory of the little girl with the violet eyes, to whom he at least was bound. But a shadow was there; fantastic it seemed to me at first, too grotesque to be met with argument, but in whose very lack of substance, as I came to see, lay its ultimate strength. The notion of the woman, which now she was, came between him and the girl whom he had loved, whom he still loved with passion, and separated them. It was only on our voyage home, when we walked the deck together interminably during the hot, sleepless nights, that he first revealed to me without subterfuge, the slow agony by which this phantom slew him. And his old bitter conviction of the malignity of his luck, which had lain dormant in the first flush of his material prosperity, returned to him. The apparent change in it seemed to him just then, the last irony of those hostile powers which had pursued him.

'It came to me suddenly,' he said, 'just before I left Agnas, when I had been adding up my pile and saw there was nothing to keep me, that it was all wrong. I had been a blamed fool! I might have gone home years ago. Where is the best of my life? Burnt out, wasted, buried in that cursed oven! Dollars? If I had all the metal in Chili, I couldn't buy one day of youth. Her youth too; that has gone with the rest; that's the worst part!'

Despite all my protests, his despondency increased as the steamer ploughed her way towards England, with the ceaseless throb of her screw, which was like the panting of a great beast. Once, when we had been talking of other matters, of certain living poets whom he favoured, he broke off with a quotation from the 'Prince's Progress' of Miss Rossetti:

> 'Ten years ago, five years ago,
>   One year ago,
> Even then you had arrived in time,
>   Though somewhat slow;
> Then you had known her living face
>   Which now you cannot know.'

He stopped sharply, with a tone in his voice which seemed to intend, in the lines, a personal instance.

'I beg your pardon!' I protested. 'I don't see the analogy. You haven't loitered; you don't come too late. A brave woman has waited for you; you have a fine felicity before you: it should be all the better, because you have won it laboriously. For Heaven's sake, be reasonable!' He shook his head sadly; then added, with a gesture of sudden passion, looking out over the taffrail, at the heaving gray waters: 'It's finished. I haven't any longer the courage.' 'Ah!' I exclaimed impatiently, 'say once for all, outright, that you are tired of her, that you want to back out of it.' 'No,' he said drearily, 'it isn't that. I can't reproach myself with the least wavering. I have had a single passion; I have given my life to it; it is there still, consuming me. Only the girl I loved: it's as if she had died. Yes, she is dead, as dead as Helen: and I have not the consolation of knowing where they have laid her. Our marriage will be a ghastly mockery: a marriage of corpses. Her heart, how can she give it me? She gave it years ago to the man I was, the man who is dead. We, who are left, are nothing to one another, mere strangers.'

One could not argue with a perversity so infatuate: it was useless to point out, that in life a distinction so arbitrary as the one which haunted him does not exist. It was only left me to wait, hoping that in the actual event of their meeting, his malady would be healed. But this meeting, would it ever be compassed? There were moments when his dread of it seemed to have grown so extreme, that he would be capable of any cowardice, any compromise to postpone it, to render it impossible. He was afraid that she would read his revulsion in his eyes, would suspect how time and his very constancy had given her the one rival with whom she could never compete; the memory of her old self, of her gracious girlhood, which was dead. Might not she too, actually, welcome a reprieve; however readily she would have submitted, out of honour or lassitude, to a marriage which could only be a parody of what might have been?

At Lisbon, I hoped that he had settled these questions, had grown reasonable and sane, for he wrote a long letter to her which was subsequently a matter of much curiosity to me; and he wore, for a day or two afterwards, an air almost of assurance which deceived me. I wondered what he had put in that epistle, how far he had explained himself, justified his curious attitude. Or was it simply a *résumé*, a conclusion to those many letters which he had written at Agnas Blancas, the last one which he would ever address to the little girl of the earlier photograph?

Later, I would have given much to decide this, but she herself, the woman who read it, maintained unbroken silence. In return, I kept a secret from her, my private interpretation of the accident of his death. It seemed to me a knowledge tragical enough for her, that he should have died as he did, so nearly in English waters; within a few days of the home coming, which they had passionately expected for years.

It would have been mere brutality to afflict her further, by lifting the veil of obscurity, which hangs over that calm, moonless night, by pointing to the note of intention in it. For it is in my experience, that accidents so opportune do not in real life occur, and I could not forget that, from Garth's point of view, death was certainly a solution. Was it not, moreover, precisely a solution, which so little time before he had the appearance of having found? Indeed when the first shock of his death was past, I could feel that it was after all a solution: with his 'luck' to handicap him, he had perhaps avoided worse things than the death he met. For the luck of such a man, is it not his temperament, his character? Can any one escape from that? May it not have been an escape for the poor devil himself, an escape too for the woman who loved him, that he chose to drop down, fathoms down, into the calm, irrecoverable depths of the Atlantic, when he did, bearing with him at least an unspoilt ideal and leaving her a memory that experience could never tarnish, nor custom stale?

APPLE BLOSSOM IN BRITTANY

APPLE BLOSSOM IN BRITTANY

I

It was the feast of the Assumption in Ploumariel, at the hottest part of the afternoon. Benedict Campion, who had just assisted at vespers, in the little dove-cotted church – like everything else in Ploumariel, even vespers were said earlier than is the usage in towns – took up his station in the market-place to watch the procession pass by. The head of it was just then emerging into the Square: a long file of men from the neighbouring villages, bare-headed and chaunting, followed the crucifer. They were all clad in the picturesque garb of the Morbihan peasantry, and were many of them imposing, quite noble figures with their clear-cut Breton features, and their austere type of face. After them a troop of young girls, with white veils over their heads, carrying banners – children from the convent school of the Ursulines; and then, two and two in motley assemblage (peasant women with their white coifs walking with the wives and daughters of prosperous *bourgeois* in costumes more civilised but far less pictorial) half the inhabitants of Ploumariel – all, indeed, who had not, with Campion, preferred to be spectators, taking refuge from a broiling sun under the grateful shadow

85

of the chestnuts in the market-place. Last of all a muster of clergy, four or five strong, a small choir of bullet-headed boys, and the Curé of the parish himself, Monsieur Letêtre chaunting from his book, who brought up the rear.

Campion, leaning against his chestnut tree, watched them defile. Once a smile of recognition flashed across his face, which was answered by a girl in the procession. She just glanced from her book, and the smile with which she let her eyes rest upon him for a moment, before she dropped them, did not seem to detract from her devotional air. She was very young and slight – she might have been sixteen – and she had a singularly pretty face; her white dress was very simple, and her little straw hat, but both of these she wore with an air which at once set her apart from her companions, with their provincial finery and their rather commonplace charms. Campion's eyes followed the little figure until it was lost in the distance, disappearing with the procession down a by-street on its return journey to the church. And after they had all passed, the singing, the last verse of the 'Ave Maris Stella,' was borne across to him, through the still air, the voices of children pleasantly predominating. He put on his hat at last, and moved away; every now and then he exchanged a greeting with somebody – the communal doctor, the mayor; while here and there a woman explained him to her gossip in whispers as he passed, 'It is the Englishman of Mademoiselle Marie-Ursule – it is M. le Curé's guest.' It was to the dwelling of M. le Curé, indeed, that Campion now made his way. Five minutes' walk brought him to it; an unpretentious white house, lying back in its large garden, away from the dusty road. It was an untidy garden, rather useful than ornamental; a very little shade was offered by one incongruous plane-tree, under which a wooden table was placed and some chairs. After *déjeuner*, on those hot August days, Campion and the Curé took their- coffee here; and in the evening it was here that they sat and talked while Mademoiselle Hortense, the Curé's sister, knitted, or appeared to knit, an interminable shawl; the young girl, Marie-Ursule, placidly completing the quartet with her silent, felicitous smile of a convent-bred child, which seemed sometimes, at least to Campion, to be after all a finer mode of conversation. He threw himself down now on the bench, wondering when his hosts would have finished their devotions, and drew a book from his pocket as if he would read. But he did not open it, but sat for a long time holding it idly in his hand, and gazing out at the village, at the expanse of dark pine-covered hills, and at the one trenchant object in the foreground, the white façade of the convent of the Ursuline nuns. Once and again he smiled, as though his thoughts, which had wandered a long way, had fallen upon extraordinarily pleasant things. He was a man of barely forty, though he looked slightly older than his age: his little, peaked beard was grizzled, and a life spent in literature, and very studiously, had given him the scholar's premature stoop. He was not handsome, but, when he smiled, his smile was so pleasant that people credited him with good looks. It brought, moreover, such a light of youth into his eyes, as to suggest that if his avocations had unjustly aged his body, that had not been without its compensations – his soul had remained remarkably young. Altogether, he looked shrewd, kindly and successful, and he was all these things, while if there was also a certain sadness in his eyes – lines of lassitude about his mouth – this was an idiosyncracy of his temperament, and hardly justified by his history, which had always been honourable and smooth. He was sitting in the same calm and presumably agreeable reverie, when the garden gate opened, and a girl – the young girl of the procession, fluttered towards him.

'Are you quite alone?' she asked brightly, seating herself at his side. 'Has not Aunt Hortense come back?'

Campion shook his head, and she continued speaking in English, very correctly, but with a slight accent, which gave to her pretty young voice the last charm.

'I suppose she has gone to see *la mère Guémené*. She will not live another night they say. Ah! what a pity,' she cried, clasping her hands; 'to die on the Assumption – that is hard.'

Campion smiled softly. 'Dear child, when one's time comes, when one is old as that, the day does not matter much.' Then he went on: 'But how is it you are back; were you not going to your nuns?'

She hesitated a moment. 'It is your last day, and I wanted to make tea for you. You have had no tea this year. Do you think I have forgotten how to make it, while you have been away, as I forget my English words?'

'It's I who am forgetting such an English habit,' he protested. 'But run away and make it, if you like. I am sure it will be very good.'

She stood for a moment looking down at him, her fingers smoothing a little bunch of palest blue ribbons on her white dress. In spite of her youth, her brightness, the expression of her face in repose was serious and thoughtful, full of unconscious wistfulness. This, together with her placid manner, the manner of a child who has lived chiefly with old people and quiet nuns, made her beauty to Campion a peculiarly touching thing. Just then her eyes fell upon Campion's wide-awake, lying on the seat at his side, and travelled to his uncovered head. She uttered a protesting cry: 'Are you not afraid of a *coup de soleil*? See – you are not fit to be a guardian if you can be so foolish as that. It is I who have to look after you.' She took up the great grey hat and set it daintily on his head; then with a little laugh she disappeared into the house.

When Campion raised his head again, his eyes were smiling, and in the light of a sudden flush which just died out of it, his face looked almost young.

II

This girl, so foreign in her education and traditions, so foreign in the grace of her movements, in everything except the shade of her dark blue eyes, was the child of an English father; and she was Benedict Campion's ward. This relation, which many persons found incongruous, had befallen naturally enough. Her father had been Campion's oldest and most familiar friend; and when Richard Heath's romantic marriage had isolated him from so many others, from his family and from his native land, Campion's attachment to him had, if possible, only been increased. From his heart he had approved, had prophesied nothing but good of an alliance, which certainly, while it lasted, had been an wholly ideal relation. There had seemed no cloud on the horizon – and yet less than two years had seen the end of it. The birth of the child, Marie-Ursule, had been her mother's death; and six months later, Richard Heath, dying less from any defined malady than because he lacked any longer the necessary motive to live, was laid by the side of his wife. The helpless child remained, in the guardianship of Hortense, her mother's sister, and elder by some ten years, who had already composed herself contentedly, as some women do, to the prospect of perpetual spinsterhood, and the care of her brother's house – an ecclesiastic just appointed curé of Ploumariel. And here, ever since, in this quiet corner of Brittany, in the tranquil custody of the priest and his sister, Marie-Ursule had grown up.

Campion's share in her guardianship had not been onerous, although it was necessarily maintained; for the child had inherited, and what small property would come to her was in England, and in English funds. To Hortense Letêtre and her brother such responsibilities in an alien land were not for a moment to be entertained. And gradually, this connection, at first formal and impersonal, between Campion and the Breton presbytery, had developed into an intimacy, into a friendship singularly satisfying on both sides. Separate as their interests seemed, those of the French country-priest, and of the Englishman of letters, famous already in his own department, they had, nevertheless, much community of feeling apart from their common affection for a child. Now, for many years, he had been established in their good graces, so that it had become an habit with him to spend his holiday – it was often a very extended one – at Ploumariel; while to the Letêtres, as well as to Marie-Ursule herself, this annual sojourn of Campion's had become the occasion of the year, the one event which pleasantly relieved the monotony of life in this remote village; though that, too, was a not unpleasant routine. Insensibly Campion had come to find his chief pleasure in consideration of this child of an old friend, whose gradual growth beneath influences which seemed to him singularly exquisite and fine, he had watched so long; whose future, now that her childhood, her schooldays at the convent had come to an end, threatened to occupy him with an anxiety more intimate than any which hitherto he had known. Marie-Ursule's future! They had talked much of it that summer, the priest and the Englishman, who accompanied him in his long morning walks, through green lanes, and over white, dusty roads, and past fields perfumed with the pungently pleasant smell of the blood-red *sarrasin*, when he paid visits to the sick who lived on the outskirts of his scattered parish. Campion became aware then of an increasing difficulty in discussing this matter impersonally, in the impartial manner becoming a guardian. Odd thrills of jealousy stirred within him when he was asked to contemplate Marie-Ursule's possible suitors. And yet, it was with a very genuine surprise, at least for the moment, that he met the Curé's sudden pressing home of a more personal contingency – he took this freedom of an old friend with a shrewd twinkle in his eye, which suggested that all along this had been chiefly in his mind. '*Mon bon ami*, why should you not marry her yourself? That would please all of us so much.' And he insisted, with kindly insistence, on the propriety of the thing: dwelling on Campion's established position, their long habit of friendship, his own and his sister's confidence and esteem, taking for granted, with that sure insight which is the gift of many women and of most priests, that on the ground of affection alone the justification was too obvious to be pressed. And he finished with a smile, stopping to take a pinch of snuff with a sigh of relief – the relief of a man who has at least seasonably unburdened himself.

'Surely, *mon ami*, some such possibility must have been in your mind?'

Campion hesitated for a moment; then he proffered his hand, which the other warmly grasped. 'You read me aright,' he said slowly, 'only I hardly realised it before. Even now – no, how can I believe it possible – that she should care for me. *Non sum dignus, non sum dignus*. Consider her youth, her inexperience; the best part of my life is behind me.'

But the Curé smiled reassuringly. 'The best part is before you,

Campion; you have the heart of a boy. Do we not know you? And for the child – rest tranquil there! I have the word of my sister, who is a wise woman, that she is sincerely attached to you; not to speak of the evidence of my own eyes. She will be seventeen shortly, then she can speak for herself. And to whom else can we trust her?'

The shadow of these confidences hung over Campion when he next saw Marie-Ursule, and troubled him vaguely during the remainder of his visit, which this year, indeed, he considerably curtailed. Inevitably he was thrown much with the young girl, and if daily the charm which he found in her presence was sensibly increased, as he studied her from a fresh point of view, he was none the less disquieted at the part which he might be called upon to play. Diffident and scrupulous, a shy man, knowing little of women; and at least by temperament, a sad man, he trembled before felicity, as many at the palpable breath of misfortune. And his difficulty was increased by the conviction, forced upon him irresistibly, little as he could accuse himself of vanity, that the decision rested with himself. Her liking for him was genuine and deep, her confidence implicit. He had but to ask her and she would place her hand in his and go forth with him, as trustfully as a child. And when they came to celebrate her *fête*, Marie-Ursule's seventeenth birthday – it occurred a little before the Assumption – it was almost disinterestedly that he had determined upon his course. At least it was security which he could promise her, as a younger man might not; a constant and single-minded kindness; a devotion not the less valuable, because it was mature and reticent, lacking, perhaps, the jealous ardours of youth. Nevertheless, he was going back to England without having revealed himself; there should be no unseasonable haste in the matter; he would give her another year. The Curé smiled deprecatingly at the procrastination; but on this point Campion was firm. And on this, his last evening, he spoke only of trivial things to Marie-Ursule, as they sat presently over the tea – a mild and flavourless beverage – which the young girl had prepared. Yet he noticed later, after their early supper, when she strolled up with him to the hill overlooking the village, a certain new shyness in her manner, a shadow, half timid, half expectant in her clear eyes which permitted him to believe that she was partly prepared. When they reached the summit, stood clear of the pine trees by an ancient stone Calvary, Ploumariel lay below them, very fair in the light of the setting sun; and they stopped to rest themselves, to admire.

'Ploumariel is very beautiful,' said Campion after a while. 'Ah! Marie-Ursule, you are fortunate to be here.'

'Yes.' She accepted his statement simply, then suddenly: 'You should not go away.' He smiled, his eyes turning from the village in the valley to rest upon her face: after all, she was the daintiest picture, and Ploumariel with its tall slate roofs, its sleeping houses; her appropriate frame.

'I shall come back, I shall come back,' he murmured. She had gathered a bunch of ruddy heather as they walked, and her fingers played with it now nervously. Campion stretched out his hand for it. She gave it to him without a word.

'I will take it with me to London,' he said; 'I will have Morbihan in my rooms.'

'It will remind you – make you think of us sometimes?'

For answer he could only touch her hand lightly with his lips. 'Do you think that was necessary?' And they resumed their homeward way silently, although to both of them the air seemed heavy with unspoken words.

III

When he was in London – and it was in London that for nine months out of the twelve Benedict Campion was to be found – he lived in the Temple, at the top of Hare Court, in the very same rooms in which he had installed himself, years ago, when he gave up his Oxford fellowship, electing to follow the profession of letters. Returning there from Ploumariel, he resumed at once, easily, his old avocations. He had always been a secluded man, living chiefly in books and in the past; but this year he seemed less than ever inclined to knock at the hospitable doors which were open to him. For in spite of his reserve, his diffidence, Campion's success might have been social, had he cared for it, and not purely academic. His had come to be a name in letters, in the higher paths of criticism; and he had made no enemies. To his success indeed, gradual and quiet as this was, he had never grown quite accustomed, contrasting the little he had actually achieved with all that he had desired to do. His original work was of the slightest, and a book that was in his head he had never found time to write. His name was known in other ways, as a man of ripe knowledge, of impeccable taste; as a born editor of choice reprints, of inaccessible classics: above all, as an authority – the greatest, upon the literature and the life (its flavour at once courtly, and mystical, had to him an unique charm) of the seventeenth century. His heart was in that age, and from much lingering over it, he had come to view modern life with a curious detachment, a sense of remote hostility: Democracy, the Salvation Army, the novels of M. Zola – he disliked them an impartially. A Catholic by long inheritance, he held his religion for something more than an heirloom; he exhaled it, like an intimate quality; his mind being essentially of that kind to which a mystical view of things comes easiest.

This year passed with him much as any other of the last ten years had passed; at least the routine of his daily existence admitted little outward change. And yet inwardly, he was conscious of alteration, of a certain quiet illumination which was a new thing to him.

Although at Ploumariel when the prospect of such a marriage had dawned on him, his first impression had been one of strangeness, he could reflect now that it was some such possibility as this which he had always kept vaguely in view. He had prided himself upon few things more than his patience; and now it appeared that this was to be rewarded; he was glad that he had known how to wait. This girl, Marie-Ursule, had an immense personal charm for him, but, beyond that, she was representative – her traditions were exactly those which the ideal girl of Campion's imagination would possess. She was not only personally adorable; she was also generically of the type which he admired. It was possibly because this type was, after all, so rare, that looking back, Campion in his middle age, could drag out of the recesses or his memory no spectre to compete with her. She was his first love precisely because the conditions, so choice and admirable, which rendered it inevitable for him to love her, had never occurred before. And he could watch the time of his probation gliding away with a pleased expectancy which contained no alloy of impatience. An illumination – a quite tranquil illumination: yes, it was under some such figure, without heart-burning, or adolescent fever, that love as it came to Campion was best expressed. Yet if this love was lucent rather than turbulent, that it was also deep he could remind himself, when a letter from the priest, while the spring was yet young, had sent him to Brittany, a month or two before his accustomed time, with an anxiety that was not solely due to bewilderment.

'*Our child is well, mon bon,*' so he wrote. '*Do not alarm yourself. But it will be good for you to come, if it be only because of an idea that she has, that you may remove. An idea! Call it rather a fancy – at least your coming will dispel it. Petites entêtées: I have no patience with these mystical little girls.*'

His musings on the phrase, with its interpretation varying to his mood, lengthened his long sea-passage, and the interminable leagues of railway which separated him from Pontivy, whence he had still some twenty miles to travel by the *Courrier*, before he reached his destination. But at Pontivy, the round, ruddy face of M. Letêtre greeting him on the platform dispelled any serious misgiving. Outside the post-office the familiar conveyance awaited them: its yellow inscription 'Pontivy-Ploumariel,' touched Campion electrically, as did the cheery greeting of the driver, which was that of an old friend. They shared the interior of the rusty trap – a fossil among vehicles – they chanced to be the only travellers, and to the accompaniment of jingling harness, and the clattering hoofs of the brisk little Carhaix horses, M. Letêtre explained himself.

'A vocation, *mon Dieu!* if all the little girls who fancied themselves with one, were to have their way, to whom would our poor France look for children? They are good women, *nos Ursulines*, ah, yes; but our Marie-Ursule is a good child, and blessed matrimony also is a sacrament. You shall talk to her, my Campion. It is a little fancy, you see, such as will come to young girls; a convent ague, but when she sees you' . . . He took snuff with emphasis, and flipped his broad fingers suggestively. '*Craque!* it is a betrothal, and a *trousseau*, and not the habit of religion, that Mademoiselle is full of. You will talk to her?'

Campion assented silently, absently, his eyes had wandered away, and looked through the little square of window at the sad-coloured Breton country, at the rows of tall poplars, which guarded the miles of dusty road like sombre sentinels. And the priest with a reassured air pulled out his breviary, and began to say his office in an imperceptible undertone. After a while he crossed himself, shut the book, and pillowing his head against the hot, shiny leather of the carriage, sought repose; very soon his regular, stertorous breathing, assured his companion that he was asleep. Campion closed his eyes also, not indeed in search of slumber, though he was travel weary; rather the better to isolate himself with the perplexity of his own thoughts. An indefinable sadness invaded him, and he could envy the priest's simple logic, which gave such short shrift to obstacles that Campion, with his subtle melancholy, which made life to him almost morbidly an affair of fine shades and nice distinctions, might easily exaggerate.

Of the two, perhaps the priest had really the more secular mind, as it certainly excelled Campion's in that practical wisdom, or common sense, which may be of more avail than subtlety in the mere economy of life. And what to the Curé was a simple matter enough, the removal of an idle fancy of a girl, might be to Campion, in his scrupulous temper, and his overweening tenderness towards just those pieties and renunciations which such a fancy implied, a task to be undertaken hardly with relish, perhaps without any real conviction, deeply as his personal wishes might be implicated in success. And the heart had gone out of his journey long before a turn of the road brought them in sight of Ploumariel.

IV

Up by the great, stone Calvary, where they had climbed nearly a year before, Campion stood, his face deliberately averted, while the young girl uttered her hesitating confidences; hesitating, yet candid, with a candour which seemed to separate him from the child by more than a measurable space of years, to set him with an appealing trustfulness in the seat of judgment – for him, for her. They had wandered there insensibly, through apple-orchards white with the promise of a bountiful harvest, and up the pine-clad hill, talking of little things – trifles to beguile their way – perhaps, in a sort of vain procrastination. Once, Marie-Ursule had plucked a branch of the snowy blossom, and he had playfully chided her that the cider would be less by a litre that year in Brittany. 'But the blossom is so much prettier,' she protested; 'and there will be apples and apples – always enough apples. But I like the blossom best – and it is so soon over.'

And then, emerging clear of the trees, with Ploumariel lying in its quietude in the serene sunshine below them, a sudden strenuousness had supervened, and the girl had unburdened herself, speaking tremulously, quickly, in an undertone almost passionate; and Campion, perforce, had listened. . . . A fancy? a whim? Yes, he reflected; to the normal, entirely healthy mind, any choice of exceptional conditions, any special self-consecration or withdrawal from the common lot of men and women must draw down upon it some such reproach, seeming the mere pedantry of inexperience. Yet, against his reason, and what he would fain call his better judgment, something in his heart of hearts stirred sympathetically with this notion of the girl. And it was no fixed resolution, no deliberate justification which she pleaded. She was soft, and pliable, and even her plea for renunciation contained pretty, feminine inconsequences; and it touched Campion strangely. Argument he could have met with argument; an ardent conviction he might have assailed with pleading; but that note of appeal in her pathetic young voice, for advice, for sympathy, disarmed him.

'Yet the world,' he protested at last, but half-heartedly, with a sense of self-imposture: 'the world, Marie-Ursule, it has its disappointments; but there are compensations.'

'I am afraid, afraid,' she murmured.

Their eyes alike sought instinctively the Convent of the Ursulines, white and sequestered in the valley – a visible symbol of security, of peace, perhaps of happiness.

'Even there they have their bad days: do not doubt it.'

'But nothing happens,' she said simply; 'one day is like another. They can never be very sad, you know.'

They were silent for a time: the girl, shading her eyes with one small white hand, continued to regard the convent; and Campion considered her fondly.

'What can I say?' he exclaimed at last. 'What would you put on me? Your uncle – he is a priest – surely the most natural adviser – you know his wishes.'

She shook her head. 'With him it is different – I am one of his family – he is not a priest for me. And he considers me a little girl – and yet I am old enough to marry. Many young girls have had a vocation before my age. Ah, help me, decide for me!' she pleaded; 'you are my *tuteur.*'

'And a very old friend, Marie-Ursule.' He smiled rather sadly. Last year seemed so long ago, and the word, which he had almost spoken then, was no longer seasonable. A note in his voice, inexplicable, might have touched her. She took his hand impulsively, but he withdrew it quickly, as though her touch had scalded him.

'You look very tired; you are not used to our Breton rambles in this sun. See, I will run down to the cottage by the chapel and fetch you some milk. Then you shall tell me.'

When he was alone the smile faded from his face and was succeeded by a look of lassitude, as he sat himself beneath the shadow of the Calvary to wrestle with his responsibility. Perhaps it was a vocation: the phrase, sounding strangely on modern ears, to him, at least, was no anachronism. Women of his race, from generation to generation, had heard some such voice and had obeyed it. That it went unheeded now was, perhaps, less a proof that it was silent, than that people had grown hard and deaf, in a world that had deteriorated. Certainly the convent had to him no vulgar, Protestant significance, to be combated for its intrinsic barbarism; it suggested nothing cold nor narrow nor mean, was veritably a gracious choice, a generous effort after perfection. Then it was for his own sake, on an egoistic impulse, that he should dissuade her? And it rested with him; he had no doubt that he could mould her, even yet, to his purpose. The child! how he loved her. . . . But would it ever be quite the same with them after that morning? Or must there be henceforth a shadow between them; the knowledge of something missed, of the lower end pursued, the higher slighted? Yet, if she loved him? He let his head drop on his hands, murmured aloud at the hard chance which made him at once judge and advocate in his own cause. He was not conscious of praying, but his mind fell into that condition of aching blankness which is, perhaps, an extreme prayer. Presently he looked down again at Ploumariel, with its coronal of faint smoke ascending in the perfectly still air, at the white convent of the Dames Ursulines, which seemed to dominate and protect it. How peaceful it was! And his thought wandered to London: to its bustle and noise, its squalid streets, to his life there, to its literary coteries, its politics, its society; vulgar and trivial and sordid they all seemed from this point of vantage. That was the world he had pleaded for, and it was into that he would bring the child. . . . And suddenly, with a strange reaction, he was seized with a sense of the wisdom of her choice, its pictorial fitness, its benefit for both of them. He felt at once and finally, that he acquiesced in it; that any other ending to his love had been an impossible grossness, and that to lose her in just that fashion was the only way in which he could keep her always. And his acquiescence was without bitterness, and attended only by that indefinable sadness which to a man of his temper was but the last refinement of pleasure. He had renounced, but he had triumphed; for it seemed to him that his renunciation would be an ægis to him always against the sordid facts of life, a protest against the vulgarity of instinct, the tyranny of institutions. And he thought of the girl's life, as it should be, with a tender appreciation – as of something precious laid away in lavender. He looked up to find her waiting before him with a basin half full of milk, warm still, fresh from the cow; and she watched him in silence while he drank. Then their eyes met, and she gave a little cry.

'You will help me? Ah, I see that you will! And you think I am right?'

'I think you are right, Marie-Ursule.'

'And you will persuade my uncle?'

'I will persuade him.'

She took his hand in silence, and they stood so for a minute, gravely regarding each other. Then they prepared to descend.

THE EYES OF PRIDE

THE EYES OF PRIDE

To A.F.

> *'Pluck out the eyes of pride; thy lips to mine?*
> *Never, though I die thirsting! Go thy ways!'*

GEORGE MEREDITH

I

'Do as you please – it's all one to me: yet I think you will live to regret it.'

He spoke sullenly, with well-affected indifference, standing on the hearth-rug, his hands in his pockets, looking down at her; and yet there was a note of irresolution, of potential suffering in his voice, which was absent from her reply:

'If I do, I will tell you.'

'That is just what you will never do.'

'Perhaps not.' She was actually indifferent, or her dissimulation was more profound than his, for the blank coldness of her speech lit a spark of irritation in him.

'And, all the same, I think you will regret it — every day of your life. . . . By God! you are making a great mistake, Rosalind!'

'Is it all coming over again?' murmured the girl, wearily. 'And, after all, it's your own choice.'

He flushed angrily. He was in evening dress, and he fidgeted with his tie for a moment, before he held out his hand with stiff courtesy.

'Good-bye,' he said; and 'Good-bye, Mr. Seefang!' the girl answered, listlessly. He dropped her impassive hand, and went slowly towards the door. Then he remembered he had brought his hat with him into the drawing-room, and he came back again, and placed it mechanically under his arm. 'Well, good-bye, Rosalind!' he said again This time she made no response, and he was really gone when she raised her eyes again. . . .

When he opened the hall door, emerged into the square, he paused to light a cigar before he plunged into the fog, rank and yellow and raw, which engulfed him. A clock struck eleven. It was actually so late; and he began to look round, vaguely, for a hansom, reflecting that their rapid talk – certainly, it had been fruitful in momentous consequences – had lasted for over an hour. He decided that all the cabs would have disappeared; the square railings, ten yards in front of him, were invisible; he shrugged his shoulders – a gesture habitual with him, in which, just now, lassitude and a certain relief were mingled – and, doggedly and resolutely, he set his face eastwards, to accomplish on foot his return journey to the Temple. . . . As he went, his mind was recasting his past life, and more especially the last six months of it, during which he had been engaged to Rosalind Lingard. Well! that was over at last, and he was unable to add that it had been pleasant while it lasted. Pleasant? Well, no! but it had been an intoxicating experience – a delirious torture. Now he was a free man, and he tried to congratulate himself, reminding himself of all the phrase implied. Yes; he was free again – free to his old pleasures and his old haunts, to his friends and his former wandering life, if he chose; above all, free to his art – his better passion. . . . And, suddenly, into his meditation there floated the face of the girl on the sofa, impassively beautiful and sullen, as it had been framed to his vision when he last held her hand, and he ground his teeth and cursed aloud.

He began to remember how, all along, he had forecasted this end of

his wooing. What an ill-omened affair it had been from the first! He
was yet uncertain whether he loved or hated her most. That he had
loved her at all was the miracle. But, even now, he knew that he had
loved her, with a love that was not child's-play – it had come too late
for that – but, like his genius, faulty yet tremendous.

There was a great deal of Seefang; even the critics of his pictures
admitted it, and everything about him was on a large scale. So that
when he had fallen in love with Rosalind Lingard, after three days'
acquaintance, he had done so supremely, carried away by a strange
hurricane of sensual fascination and spiritual rapture. Meeting her first
at a sparsely-attended *table d'hôte* in a primitive Breton village where
he was painting, he had promptly disliked her, thought her capricious
and ill-tempered. Grudgingly, he had admitted that she was beautiful,
but it was a beauty which repelled him in a girl of his own class,
although he would have liked it well enough in women of less title to
respect, with whom he was far too well acquainted.

If he had ever thought of marriage – and it must have been remotely
– during his fifteen years of manhood, spent so pleasantly in the practice
of an art in which his proficiency had met recognition and in the frank
and unashamed satisfaction of his vigorous appetites, he had dreamed
of a girl most unlike Rosalind Lingard; a girl with the ambered paleness
and the vaguely virginal air of an early Tuscan painting, who would
cure him of his grossness and reform him. For he had, still, intervals of
depression – generally when he had spoiled a canvas – in which he
accused himself of living like a beast, and hankered, sentimentally, for
the love of a good woman. And yet, Rosalind Lingard, with her
ambiguous charm, her adorable imperfection, had been this woman –
the first to dominate him by something more than the mere rose and
white of her flesh. Masterful as he had been with the others, he was her
slave, if it was still his masterfulness which bound her to him, for a
pliant man would have repelled her, and she had dreamed of being
loved tyrannically. A few days had sufficed. A juxtaposition somewhat
out of the common – a slight illness of her aunt, Mrs. Sartorys, with
whom she was travelling – having thrown them together, a discovery

which he made suddenly, that if she was capricious she could yet be charming, and that her audacity was really the perfection of her innocence – these were the material agents of his subjection. To the lovers, as they became speedily, inevitable fate and the god who watches over little lovers were held alone responsible. The best of Seefang's character, in which the fine and the gross were so strangely mingled, leapt to meet the promise in her eyes. Their vows were exchanged. . . .

He crossed Piccadilly Circus, debating whether he should go home at once or turn into his club and have an hour's poker; finally, he decided to make for the Temple. . . . And he told himself again that it was over. In retrospect, their love seemed like a long quarrel, with a few intervals of reconciliation. But there had been a time, at the very beginning, when life was like Eden; when he was so buoyant that he felt as if his head must touch the sky. He left his easel and wandered with them through Morbihan; his knowledge of the country, so sad and cold and poor, and yet so pictorial, made him their *cicerone* to nooks which elude the ordinary tourist. Actually, they were not betrothed, but they anticipated the official sanction; and, indeed, no opposition was expected even by Mrs. Sartorys; though, formally, Rosalind's guardian, a learned lawyer – an abstract idea, even, to his ward – was to be consulted. Seefang had his fame, his kinship with the peerage, to set off against the girl's fortune, which was considerable. Had he been less eligible, Mrs. Sartorys, a weak, placid woman, professionally an invalid, would have been equally submissive. As it was, she allowed them the license of an engagement, stipulating merely for a postponement which was nominal. They rambled alone together over the ruddy moorland as it pleased them. Once he said to her:

'If your guardian damns me, will you make a curtsy and dismiss me, Rosalind?'

They had come to a pause in their walk; the sun was merciless, and they had wandered off the road to seek shade; the girl had seated herself on a bank under a silver-birch tree, Seefang was standing over her. She shook her head.

'No! if I've ever wanted anything since I was a child, I've cried and stormed till I got it.'

'You give yourself a fine character.'

'I'm not a nice girl, I've told you so before.'

'Nice!' he looked at her gravely. 'I don't care about niceness.'

'What do you care for?'

'You as you are,' he said deliberately; 'proud, capricious, not very sweet of temper, and – I suspect –'

Her eyes challenged him, he completed his phrase: 'A bit of a flirt!'

'And yet you –'

'And yet I love you; good God! what am I myself?'

She glanced at him with a sort of mocking tenderness.

'You are very proud,' she said; 'capricious, I don't know; but stubborn and headstrong; I think you can be very cruel, and I am sure you have been very wicked.'

'And yet? –' he imitated her phrase softly. They were quite alone with the trees and the birds, and instinctively their lips met. Presently she resumed, a trifle sadly, her eyes contemplating vaguely the distant valley.

'I'm only a girl – not twenty. You are thirty-eight, thirty-eight! You must have kissed so many, many women before me.'

He touched her hand very softly, held it while he went on: 'Never mind the past, Rosalind. I've lived as other men. If I've been stupid, it was because I had never known you. When a man has been in heaven he is in no hurry to get back anywhere else. I'm yours, and you know it – body and soul – and they are a poor bargain, my child! ever since – since Ploumariel.' She flushed and her head drooped towards him; at Ploumariel they had crossed the great climacteric. When she looked up, the sun, moving westwards, lit up the valley opposite them, illuminated the white stones of a village cemetery. Her eyes rested upon it. Presently she said:

'Oh, my dear, let us be kind to each other, bear and forbear. . . . That's the end of it all.'

For a moment he was silent; then he leant over and kissed her hair.

'Rosalind, my darling, I wish we were dead together, you and I, lying there quietly, out of the worry of things.'

It was a fantastic utterance, an odd and ominous mood to interrupt their foolish talk of plighted lovers; it never recurred. But just now it came to him like an intuition. It is so much easier to die for the woman you love than to live with her. They could talk of bearing and forbearing, but much tolerance was in the nature of neither. They were capable of generosity, but even to themselves they could not be just. Both had known speedily how it must end. He was impatient, tyrannical; she, capricious and utterly a woman; their pride was a great Juggernaut, beneath whose car they threw, one by one, their dearest hopes, their happiness and all that they cared most for in life. Was she a coquette? At least she cared for admiration, encouraged it, declined to live her life as he would have it. His conviction that small sacrifices which he asked of her she refused, not from any abiding joy the possession gave her, but in sheer perverseness, setting her will against his own, heightened his estimation of the offence. That his anger was out of all proportion to her wrongdoing he knew, and his knowledge merely inflamed his passionate resentment. She, on her side, was exacting, jealous of his past life; he was faithfully her lover, and he felt aggrieved, perhaps unjustly, that woman-like she took constancy too much for granted, was not more grateful that he did not lapse. And neither could make concessions: they hardened their hearts, were cold of eye and tongue when a seasonable softening would have flung them each in the other's arms. When they were most divided, each was secretly aware that life without the other would be but a savourless dish. For all that, they had ended it. She had flung him back his liberty, and he had accepted it with a bitter word of thanks. They had said, if they had not done, irrevocable things. . . .

Seefang let himself into his chambers and slammed the oak behind him; the room smelt of fog, the fire had gone out, and, just then, the lack of it seemed the most intolerable thing in life. But he sat down, still in his ulster, lighting the candle to dispel the gloom, and faced his freedom more deliberately than he had done before. He began to think of his work, and he was surprised at discovering how utterly he had neglected it during the last six months. There is nothing so disorganising as a great passion, nothing so enervating as a virtuous one. He went to bed, vowing that he would make amends. His art! that he should ever have forgotten it! None of the other women had interfered with that, the women who had amused him, satisfied the animal in him, but whom he had not loved. She alone had made him forget it. He had a sense of ingratitude towards his art, as to a person who has always stood by one, whom at times one has not valued, and whom one finds, after some calamity, steadfast and unchanged. His art should stand him in good stead now; it should help him to endure his life, to forget her and be strong. Strength! that was the great thing; and he knew that it appertained to him. He fell asleep murmuring that he was glad he was strong . . . . strong . . . . Two months later Seefang went abroad; he had made arrangements for a prolonged absence. He had not seen Miss Lingard; if an acquaintance, who was ignorant of the rupture, asked after her, he looked vacant, seemed to search his memory to give the name a connotation. Then he remarked indifferently that he believed Mrs. Sartorys was out of town. He was working hard, contemplated work more arduous still. Every now and then he drew himself up and reminded himself that he had forgotten her.

For two years he was hardly heard of: he was believed to be travelling in Spain, living in some secluded village. Then he was in London for a month: he exhibited, and critics were unanimous in their opinion that he had never done better work – at which he smiled. They declared he had not been in vain to the land of Velasquez and Goya. It was at this time that he heard of Miss Lingard's marriage with Lord Dagenham; that nobleman had carried away his bride to an obscure Scandinavian capital, where he was diplomatically engaged. Seefang was curious enough to turn over the pages of Debrett, and discovered that the bridegroom was sixty; it enabled him to credit the current rumour that he was dull. He went on smiling and was abroad for another three years.

II

He had known they would meet when he first heard that the Dagenhams were in town. Lord Dagenham had abandoned diplomacy with stays and any semblance of being young; he was partly paralysed, and was constantly to be seen in a bath-chair in Kensington Gardens. But the lady went everywhere, and Seefang made much the same round; their encounter was merely a question of time. He faced it with equanimity, or its tolerable imitation; he neither feared it nor hoped for it. And the season was but a few weeks old when it came about. At the dinner-table he faced her almost directly.

Five years! Her beauty was richer, perhaps; it had acquired sombre tones like an old picture; but she was not perceptibly altered, hardly older. She was straight and tall, had retained something of her slim, girlish figure; and, as of old, her beauty had a sullen stain on it; in the languid depths of her dark eyes their fate was written; her full mouth in repose was scornful. He finished his soup, talked to his neighbour, mingled in the conversation; one of his remarks sent a little ripple of well-bred laughter down the table, and he noticed that she joined in it. But her eyes avoided him, as they had done when she bowed to him formally in the drawing-room. They had not spoken. A vague feeling of irritation invaded him. Was there another woman in the world with hair like that, so dark and multitudinous? He had promised himself to forget her, and it seemed to him that the promise had been kept. Life had been amusing, full of experience, lavish and expansive. If one supreme delight were impossible, that had not seemed to him a reason for denying himself any lesser joys which offered – joys, distractions. How successful he had been! And the tide of his irritation rose higher. His mind went back to the days when he had first known her. She had forgotten them, no doubt, but they were good while they lasted – yes, they were good. But what a life they would have led! – how thankful he should have been for his escape! From time to time he fidgeted nervously with his tie. Like a great wave of anguish his old desire swept over him.

To Lady Dagenham, if she had not seemed to notice him, his presence there, facing her, was the one fact which possessed her mind during that interminable dinner-party. She had to perfection the gift of being rude urbanely, and she had begun by repressing any intentions of her neighbour on the right to be conversational. Her neighbour on the left talked for three; she preserved appearances by throwing him smiles, and at mechanical intervals an icy monosyllable. 'Yes,' and 'Yes,' said her lips, and her eyes, which looked everywhere else – above, below, beside him – saw only Seefang. . . . He was changed; older, coarser, bigger, she thought. Large he had always been; but to-night he loomed stupendous. Every now and then his deep voice was borne across to her – that remained the same, his voice was always pleasant. And she missed no detail – his hair was thinner, it was streaked, like his moustache, with gray; his eyes were clouded, a trifle blood-shot; his laugh was cynical and easy. She noticed the one ring he wore, a curious, absinthe-coloured opal, when he moved his left hand, large, but well-shaped and white. She remembered the ring and his affection for opals. Had that been the secret of his luck – their luck? He was not noticeably pitiable, but instinctively she fell to pitying him, and her compassion included herself. Skeleton fingers groped out of the past and throttled her. At a familiar gesture, when his hand went up to his tie, a rush of memories made her giddy. Was the past never done with? And why wish things undone or altered? He was a cross, brutal fellow; stupid and self-indulgent. Why had they ever met? They were too much alike. And she was sorry for him, sorry if he still cared, and sorrier if, as was more likely, he had forgotten; for she was aware that the strength which puts away suffering is more costly than acquiescence in unhappiness. A sudden tenderness came over her for him; it was not with the man she was angry, but with fate, the powers which had made them what they were, self-tormenters, the instruments of their own evil. As she rose from the table with the other women, she dropped one glance at him from her sombre, black eyes. And they met his in a flash which was electric.

When he came upstairs, rather tardily, it was with a certain relief that he failed to discover in either of the two large rooms, which opened into one another, the face which he sought. In the first of them, a young Hungarian musician of note was just taking his seat at the piano. The air was heavy with the smell of flowers, full of soft vibrations – the *frou-frou* of silken skirts, the rustle of posturing fans. He moved into the second room. It was a parched, hot night, and the windows had been left open; the thin lace curtains protecting them were stirred imperceptibly. With a strange, nervous dread on him that was also an intuition, he pushed them aside and stepped on to the spacious balcony. Half-a-dozen people were sitting or standing there, and he distinguished her profile, marble white and strangely cold, in the subdued shine of the electric lights. An elderly-looking young man with a blonde moustache was talking with her. He took his station by them, joined mechanically in the conversation, looking not at her, but at the long, low line of the park in front of them with its background of mysterious trees. Presently a crash of chords came from within – the Hungarian had begun his performance. People began to drift inside again; Lady Dagenham and the blonde young man – a little anxious, for he was due in the House, concerned for a division – were the last loiterers. For the second time their eyes met, and there was a note of appeal in them.

'Please don't let me keep you, Mr. Rose . . . Mr. Seefang . . . We are old friends, and I haven't seen him for years . . . Mr. Seefang will look after me.'

When they were alone together he came over to her side, and they stood so for a moment or two in silence; he was so close to her that he could smell the misty fragrance of her hair, hear the sighing of her bosom. The tense silence preyed on them; to break it at any cost, he said, at last: 'Rosalind!' Her white face was turned towards him, and he read the passion in it as in a book. And, 'Rosalind!' he said again, with a new accent, more strenuously.

'So you have come back' – her rich voice was under control, but there was a vibration in it which spoke of effort – 'come back to England? Your fame preceded you long ago. I have often heard of you, and wondered if we should ever meet.'

'Did you ever wish it?'

'It is always pleasant to meet old friends,' she answered mechanically.

'Pleasant!' He laughed harshly. 'There is no pleasure in it, Lady Dagenham.' She glanced at him uneasily, for, unconsciously, he had raised his voice. 'And friends, are we friends – how can we be friends, you and I?'

'At least – not enemies,' she murmured.

He was silent for a moment, looking out at the blurred mass of the park, but seeing only her face, the face of her youth, softened and idealised, so that five years seemed as yesterday, and the anger and bitterness, which had driven them apart, chimeras.

'At Ploumariel, up the hill to Sainte-Barbe'; he spoke softly, as it were to himself, and the natural harshness of his voice was modulated. 'Do you remember the wood, the smell of pines and wild thyme? The pine-needles crackled under your little feet. How warm it was! You were tired at the end of the climb; you sat on a boulder to rest, while I fetched you milk from the cottage by the chapel – fresh milk in a big, yellow bowl, too big for your little fingers to cling to. You laughed; and I held it to your mouth, and you made me drink too, and I drank where the print of your lips had been, and your lips were sweet and fresh –'

'Seefang!' she laid a white finger on his mouth, beseechingly, and he trembled; then let her hand rest on his with something of a caress. 'What is the use, Seefang? – what is the use? Do you think I have forgotten? . . . That was over and done with years and years ago. It is no use maddening ourselves. We have so little, little time. Even now, someone may interrupt us at any moment; we may not meet again – tell me about yourself, your life, all these years. I know you are a great artist; have you been happy?'

'I have made a name,' he said, shortly, 'in more than one sense. If I were to speak, my voice might lie to you. Look me in the face – that will answer you.'

Almost childishly she obeyed him, scrutinised the dark, strong face, harsh and proud, with engrained lines of bitterness and ill-temper set upon it even in repose.

'You have answered me,' she said, with a little moan.

'I have always longed for you, Rosalind, even when it seemed I had forgotten you most . . . And you –?'

She cut him short quickly.

'I have not been over happy,' she said.

'Then your husband –?'

'My husband has been kind to me. I have done – tried to do my duty to him.'

A fresh silence intervened, nervous and uneasy: each feared to dissipate it, for each was instinctively conscious of what gulfs of passion lay beneath it, irretrievable chasms into which one unstudied phrase, one word at random, might hurl them both. She was the first to make the venture.

'Can we not be friends, you and I?' And, innocently as she had spoken, the words had not fallen before she was conscious of her error; and his arms were round her, crushing the frail lace of her bodice, and their lips had joined, and the thrill in her blood had belied her protest.

'Oh, why did we do it, what was the good of it, why did we ever meet?' she moaned, when the passionate moment had passed, and they were left face to face together, stupefied, yet with the mask of convention upon them once more, if set a little awry.

'Because – because –' he faltered. 'Oh, my darling, how can we ever be friends? Oh, my love, my one love, anything but that! . . . There is only one end of it – or two – one of two, and you know that, Rosalind! My clever, cross darling, you were always clever – always understood. That is why I liked you.'

She stood free of him again; her hands deftly, nervously restored one of her black, ruffled tresses.

'How little you liked me, after all!' she said at last.

And she saw, with a keen delight in her power to hurt him, with more pain at the hurt she did herself, the harsh and sneering lines round his mouth and nostrils darken into prominence, the latent brute in his face accentuate.

'There was little enough to like in you, was there, Rosalind? But, by God! I did – I loved you, yes, I love you . . . Look at the park, Rosalind! It's a mist, and dark; you can guess at the trees, believe in the grass; perhaps it's soft – and new there – it's vague and strange . . . would you plunge into it now with me, darling – into the darkness? How this music and people tire me since I've seen you . . . would you? Cool and vague and strange! . . . No, you wouldn't – nor would I, even if it were possible. You need not answer. It would not do. There, or here, we should hurt each other as we always have – and shall, this side of the grave. That is why I said there was only one end of it, or two, and *this* is the one you choose.'

Once more, she laid her hand on his, and went on, her fingers caressing, absently, the opal of his ring.

'Don't be angry, Seefang, we have so little time – if it must be so. Life is so short. Besides, we've changed, grown older; we might be kinder to each other now. What are you going to do?'

'I shall live as I have done – go abroad, perhaps, a little sooner – what else?'

'Oh, why?' she cried instinctively. 'What is the good?'

'Would you have me come and see you? When are you at home? What is your day?' he asked, with an inflection, the irony of which escaped her.

'If you are reasonable, why not?' she queried.

He took up her hand and kissed it very gently, and, as it might have been a child's, retained it in his own.

'Because I am not that kind of man,' he said; 'because I know myself, and the world, and the world's view of me; because of my other name, out of paint; because –'

She pulled herself away, petulantly; withdrew from him with a sullen gesture.

'How little you must respect me! You need not have told me that your reputation is infamous: I have heard of it: is it true, then?'

'It is true that I love you. As for what they say –' he broke off with a little suppressed laugh. 'You see we are beginning to quarrel, we are generating a misunderstanding – and, as you said, there is so little time. The music is quite over, and we may be invaded any moment.'

'And I begin to feel chill,' she said.

He helped to arrange her cloak around her, lifted aside the curtain to allow her passage.

'So this is the end?' she said, lightly; and her subtile voice had grown expressionless.

'Yes,' he replied, dully; 'this is the very end.'

COUNTESS MARIE OF THE ANGELS

COUNTESS MARIE OF THE ANGELS

À JEAN DE TINAN

I

As he turned out of his hotel in the Avenue de l'Opéra, comparatively obscure at that hour, and emerged into the *grands boulevards,* Paris flashed upon him, all at once, her brightest illumination: row upon row of lamps tapering away in a double file to meet in a single point of light far away in the direction of the Place de la République. If it was winter by the calendar, the languid mellowness of a fine autumn lingered in the air. The Boulevard des Italiens was massed with wayfarers, sauntering, lounging with aimless and amiable nonchalance, while a gay Sunday crowd monopolized all the little tables outside the small and large cafés.

Colonel Mallory searched for a vacant place at one of them, then abandoned the search and moved slowly along, joining the rest of the throng with steps as aimless, but with sentiments somewhat remote from theirs.

Fifty, perhaps, of middle stature, his white moustache was in striking contrast with his short, crisp hair which had retained its original darkness. Obviously English, with his keen, blue eyes; obviously a soldier too, in gait and bearing, and in a certain sternness which comes of command, of high responsibility in perilous places, even when that command is kindly. An Anglo-Indian, to judge by his complexion, and the lines, tell-tale of the tropics, which scored his long, lean face, the colour of parchment. Less obviously English, and hardly military, was a certain grace, almost exotic, in his manner. He had emerged into the Boulevard Montmartre, before a café, less frequented than the others, caught his eye, and with a certain relief he could possess himself of a vacant chair on the *terrasse*. He ordered a drink, lit a cigar, and settled himself to watch with an interest which was not so much present as retrospective, the crowd of passers-by. And as he watched his eyes softened into sadness.

He had arrived from England that morning – he had not so very long arrived from India – and this crowd, these lights, the hard, bright gaiety of the boulevards was at once fantastically strange to him and strangely familiar; for, twenty, or was it nearer thirty years ago, Paris had been to him not merely the city of cities, but that one of them which most represented old associations, his adolescence, boyhood, childhood. True, there had been Les Rochers, the dilapidated château, half ruin to his recollection, and now wholly a ruin, or perhaps demolished – Les Rochers in the Vendée, where he had been born, where he had spent his summer holidays, where – how many years ago? – being at home on leave, just after he had obtained his company, he had closed the eyes of his mother.

But Paris! It was his best remembered boyhood; the interrupted studies in the Quartier, the Lycée, the boyish friendships, long since obliterated, the days of *congé* spent in the little hotel in the Rue de Varennes, where, more often than at Les Rochers, his mother, on her perpetual couch, economized her delicate days – days even then so clearly defined – as it were in an half twilight. Yes, until death and estrangement and the stern hand of circumstance had cast away that old life into the limbo of the dear irrevocable, that old life had been – Paris! Episodes the rest: the occasional visits to the relations of his

English father; and later, episodes too, London, murky London, the days at Wren's, the month or so with an army-coach at Bonn, the course at Woolwich; almost episodical too the first year of his soldiering. Quartered at Dover, what leave fell to him, he had spent in Paris – at Les Rochers sometimes, but more often at Paris – in those strangely silent rooms in the Rue de Varennes.

Looking out now, the phantasmagoria of the boulevards was obliterated and those old days floated up before him. Long before Woolwich: that time when he was a Lycéen, in the winter holidays. A vision so distinct! His mother's *salon*, the ancient, withered furniture, the faded silk of the Louis XV. chairs, the worn carpet: his mother's refined and suffering face, the quaint bird-like features of the two old Mesdemoiselles de la Touche – the near neighbours of his mother and the most intimate gossips round her couch – two ancient sisters, very noble and very withered, dating from Charles X., absorbed in good works, in the merits of their confessor, and in the exile of Frohsdorf. Very shadowy figures, more shadowy even than that of himself, in the trim uniform of his Lycée; a grave and rather silent boy, saddened by the twilight of that house, the atmosphere of his invalid mother.

More distinct was the dainty figure of a little girl, a child of fifteen, but seeming younger, united to him by a certain cousinship, remote enough to be valued, who, on her days of exit from the Sacré Cœur (his mother's constant visitor), talked with him sedately, softly – for there was a sort of hush always in that house – in an alcove of the sombre room. This child with her fragility, her face of a youthful Madonna, the decorous plaits in which her silken hair was gathered, losing thereby some of its lustre – the child seemed incongruous with and somewhat crushed and awed beneath the weight of her sonorous names: Marie-Joseph-Angèle de la Tour de Boiserie.

What did they converse of on those long and really isolated afternoons – isolated, for their elders, if they were present, and their presence overshadowed them, were really so remote, with their lives in the past, in lost things; their so little hold on, or care of, the future? But these were young, and if some of the freshness of youth had

121

been sacrificed a little to what was oppressive in their surroundings, yet they were young things, with certain common interests, and a future before them, if not of boundless possibilities, still a future.

Yet it was hardly of love which they could speak, though their kindness for each other, fostered by somewhat similar conditions, had ripened into that feeling. Of love there could be no question: for Sebastian Mallory, as for his little companion, their life, as it should be, had been already somewhat arranged. For Angèle, had not the iron-featured old grandmother, in her stately but penurious retreat near Les Rochers, resolved long ago that the shattered fortunes of a great house, so poor in all but name, were to be retrieved by a rich marriage? And for Sebastian, was not all hope of fortune centred in his adhesion to the plan which had so long been made for him: the course at Woolwich, the military career – with its prosperous probabilities beneath the protection of an influential relative – the exile, as it sometimes seemed to him then, in England? . . .

Certainly, there was much affection between these two, an affection maintained on the strength of the ambiguous cousinship, in a correspondence, scanty, but on each side sincere, for at least a few years after their roads had diverged. And there were other memories, later and more poignant, and as distinct, which surged up before his eyes; and the actual life of the boulevards grew vaguer. Had life been too much arranged for them? Had it been happier, perhaps, for him, for her, if they had been less acquiescent to circumstance, had interpreted duty, necessity – words early familiar to them – more leniently?

Colonel Mallory, at fifty, with his prosperous life behind him – and it had not been without its meed of glory – wondered to-night whether, after all, it had not been with prophetic foresight, that once, writing, in a sudden mood of despondency, more frankly than usual, to that charming friend of his boyhood, he had said, years ago:

'I feel all this is a mistake;' and, lower down in the same letter: *'Paris haunts me like a regret. I feel, as we say here, "out of it." And I fear I shall never make a good soldier. Not that I mean that I am lacking in physical courage, nor that I should disgrace myself under fire. But there is a difference*

between that and possession of the military vocation, and nature never designed me to be a man of action. . . . My mother, you, yourself, my dear, grave cousin and councillor, think much of duty, and I shall always endeavour to do mine – as circumstances have set it down for me – but there is a duty one owes to oneself, to one's character, and in that, perhaps, I have failed.'

A letter, dated 'Simla,' the last he would ever write to Mademoiselle de la Tour de Boiserie, actually, at that time, though of this fact he was ignorant, betrothed to a certain Comte Raoul des Anges. The news of the marriage reached him months later, just fresh from the excitement and tumult of a little border war, from which he had returned with a name already associated with gallantry, and a somewhat ugly wound from a Pathan spear.

In hospital, in the long nights and days, in the grievous heats, he had leisure for thought, and it is to be presumed he exercised it in a more strict analysis of his feelings, and it was certainly from this date that a somewhat stern reticence and reserve, which had always characterized his manner, became ingrained and inveterate.

And it was reticently, incidentally, and with little obvious feeling that he touched on the news in a letter to his mother:

'Et ce M. des Anges, dont je ne connais que le nom, est-il digne de notre enfant? His name at least is propitious. Tell la petite cousine – or tell her not, as you think fit, that to me she will always be "Marie of the Angels."'

II

That had seemed the end of it, of their vaguely tender and now so incongruous relation; as it was inevitably the end of their correspondence. And he set himself, buoyed up by a certain vein of austerity in his nature, to conquer that instinctive distaste which, from time to time, still exercised him towards his profession, to throw himself into its practice and theory, if not with ardour, at least with an earnestness that was its creditable imitation. And in due time he reaped his reward. . . .

But there was another memory – for the past will so very rarely bury its dead – a memory intense and incandescent, and, for all its bitterness, one which he could ill have spared.

That was five years later: invalided home, on a long leave, with a fine aroma of distinction attaching to him, it was after the funeral of his mother, after all the sad and wearisome arrangements for the disposition of Les Rochers that Colonel – then Captain – Mallory heard in Paris the loud and scandalous rumours which were associated with the figure of the Comte Raoul des Anges. There was pity mingled with the contempt with which his name was more often mentioned, for the man was young – it was his redeeming feature – but an *insensé!* It was a weakness of character (some whispered weakness of intellect) and not natural vice: so the world spoke most frequently. But his head had been turned, it had not been strong enough to support the sudden weight of his immense fortune. A great name and a colossal fortune, and *(bon garçon* though he was) the intelligence of a rabbit!

In Paris, to go no further, is there not a whole army of the shrewd, the needy, and the plausible, ready to exploit such a conjunction? And to this army of well-dressed pimps and parasites, Raoul had been an easy victim. The great name had been dragged in the mire, the colossal fortune was rapidly evaporating in the same direction, what was left of the little intelligence was debased and ruined. A marriage too early, before the lad had time to collect himself, for old Madame des Anges had kept him very tight, perhaps that had been largely responsible for the collapse. And it was said the Comtesse des Anges was little congenial, a prude, at least a *dévote*, who could hardly be expected to manage *ce pauvre Raoul*. She was little known in Paris. They were separated of course, had been for a year or more; she was living with her baby, very quietly, in some old house, which belonged to her family, at Sceaux – or was it at Fontenay-aux-Roses? – on the remnants of her own fortune.

All this, and much more, Mallory heard in club and in café during that memorable sojourn in Paris. He said nothing, but he raged in-

wardly; and one day, moved by an immense impulse of pity and tenderness, he went down to Fontenay-aux-Roses, to visit Madame des
Anges.

His visit was only for a week; that was the memory which he could
not spare, and which was yet so surpassingly bitter. He had stopped at
Sceaux, at an unpretending inn, but each day he had walked over to
Fontenay, and each day had spent many hours with her, chiefly in the
old-fashioned garden which surrounded her house. She had changed,
but she had always the same indefinable charm for him; and the virginal
purity of her noble beauty, marriage had not assailed, if it had saddened.
And if, at first, she was a little strange, gradually the recollection of
their old alliance, her consciousness of the profundity of his kindness
for her, melted the ice of their estrangement.

At last she spoke to him freely, though it had needed no speech of
hers for him to discern that she was a woman who had suffered; and in
the light of her great unhappiness, he only then saw all that she was to
him, and how much he himself had suffered.

They were very much alone. It was late in the year; the gay crowd
of the *endimanchés* had long ceased to make their weekly pilgrimages
to the enchanting suburbs which surround Paris with a veritable garden
of delight; and the smart villas on the hillside, at Sceaux and Fontenay,
were shut up and abandoned to caretakers. So that Captain Mallory
could visit the Châlet des Rosiers without exciting undue remark, or
remark that was to be accounted.

And one afternoon, as was inevitable, the flood-gates were broken
down, and their two souls looked one another in the face. But if, for
one moment, she abandoned herself, weeping pitiably on his shoulders, carried away, terrified almost by the vehemence of his passion;
for the volcanoes, which were hidden beneath the fine crust of his reticence, his self-restraint, she had but dimly suspected; it was only for a
moment. The reaction was swift and bitter; her whole life, her education, her tradition, were stronger than his protestations, stronger than
their love, their extreme sympathy, stronger than her misery. And before she had answered him – calm now, although the tears were in her

voice – he knew instinctively that she was once more far away from him, that she was not heeding his arguments, that what he had proposed was impossible; life was too strong for them. 'Leave me, my friend, my good and old friend! I was wrong – God forgive me – even to listen to you! The one thing you can do to help me, the one thing I ask of you, for the sake of our old kindness, is – to leave me.'

He had obeyed her, for the compassion, with which his love was mingled, had purged passion in him of its baser concomitants. And when the next day he had called, hardly knowing himself the object of his visit, but ready, if she still so willed it, that it should be a final one, she had not received him. . . . He was once more in India, when a packet of his old letters to her, some of them in a quite boyish handwriting, were returned to him. That she had kept them at all touched him strangely; that she should have returned them now gave him a very clear and cruel vision of how ruthlessly she would expiate the most momentary deviation from her terrible sense of duty. And the tide of his tenderness rose higher; and with his tenderness, from time to time, a certain hope, a hope which he tried to suppress, as being somewhat of a *lâcheté*, began to be mingled.

III

'*Paris haunts me like a regret!*' That old phrase, in his last letter to Mademoiselle de la Tour de Boiserie, returned to him with irony, as he sat on the boulevard, and he smiled sadly, for the charm of Paris seemed to him now like a long disused habit. Yet, after all, had he given reminiscence a chance? For it was hardly Paris of the *grands boulevards*, with its crude illumination, its hard brilliancy, its cosmopolitan life of strangers and sojourners, which his regret had implied. The Paris of his memories, the other more intimate Paris, from the Faubourg Saint Germain to the quarter of ancient, intricate streets behind the Panthéon: – there was time to visit that, to wander vaguely in the fine evening, and recall the old landmarks, if it was hardly the hour to call on Madame des Anges.

He dined at an adjacent restaurant, hastily, for time had slipped by him – then hailed a cab, which he dismissed at the Louvre, for, after the lassitude of his meditation, a feverish impulse to walk had seized him. He traversed the Place de Carrousel, that stateliest of all squares, now gaunt and cold and bare, in its white brilliance of electricity, crossed the bridge, and then striking along the Quai, found himself almost instinctively turning into the Rue du Bac. Before a certain number he came to a halt, and stood gazing up at the inexpressive windows. . . .

More than a year ago that which he had dimly hoped, and had hated himself for hoping, had befallen. The paralytic imbecile, who had dragged out an apology for a life, which at its very best would hardly have been missed, and which had been for fifteen years a burden to himself and others, the Comte Raoul des Anges, that gilded calf of a season, whose scandalous fame had long since been forgotten, was gathered to his forefathers. That news reached Colonel Mallory in India, and mechanically, and with no very definite object in his mind, yet with a distinct sense that this course was an inevitable corollary, he had handed in his papers. But some nine months later, when, relieved of his command, and gazetted as no longer of Her Majesty's service, he was once more in possession of his freedom, it was a very different man to that youthful one who had made such broken and impassioned utterances in the garden of the Châlet des Rosiers, who ultimately embarked in England.

The life, the service, for which he had retained, to the last, something of his old aversion, for which he had possessed, however well he had acquitted himself, perhaps little real capacity: all that had left its mark on him. He had looked on the face of Death, and affronted him so often, had missed him so narrowly, had seen him amid bloodshed and the clash of arms, and, with the same equanimity, in times of peace, when, yet more terribly, his angel, Cholera, devastated whole companies in a night, that life had come to have few terrors for him, and less importance.

Yet what was left of the old Sebastian Mallory was his abiding
memory, a continual sense (as it were of a spiritual presence cheering
and supporting him) of the one woman whom he had loved, whom he
still loved, if not with his youth's original ardour, yet with a great
tenderness and pity, partaking of the nature of the theological charity.

'Marie of the Angels,' as he had once in whimsical sadness called
her. Yes! He could feel now, after all those years of separation, that she
had been to him in some sort a genius actually *angelic*, affording him
just that salutary ideal, which a man needs, to carry him honourably,
or, at least, without too much self-disgust, through the miry ways of
life. And that was why, past fifty, a grim, kindly, soldierly man, he had
given up soldiering and returned to find her. That was why he stood
now in the Rue du Bac – for it was from there, on hearing of his intention,
she had addressed him – gazing up in a sentimentality almost boyish,
at those blank, unlit windows.

IV

Those windows, so cold and irresponsive, he could explain, when,
returning to his hotel, he found a note from her. It was dated from the
Châlet des Rosiers. She was so little in Paris, that she had thoughts of
letting her house; but, to meet an old and valued friend, she would
gladly have awaited him there – only, her daughter (she was still at the
Sacré Cœur, although it was her last term) had been ailing. Paris did
not agree with the child, and, perforce, she had been obliged to go
down to Fontenay to prepare for her reception. There, at any time, was
it necessary to say it? she would be glad, oh, so glad, to receive him!
There was sincerity in this letter, which spoke of other things, of his
life, and his great success – had she not read of him in the papers?
There was affection, too, between the somewhat formal lines, reticent
but real; so much was plain to him. But the little note struck chill to
him; it caused him to spend a night more troubled and painful than

was his wont – for he slept as a rule the sleep of the old campaigner, and his trouble was the greater because of his growing suspicion, that, after all, the note which Madame des Anges had struck was the true one, for both of them; that a response to it in any other key would be factitious, and that his pilgrimage was a self-deception. And this impression was only heightened when, on the morrow, he made his way to the station of the Luxembourg, which had been erected long since his day, when the facilities of travel were less frequent, and took his ticket for Fontenay. So many thousand miles he had come to see her, and already a certain vague terror of his approaching interview was invading him. Ah! if it had been Paris! . . . But here, at Fontenay-aux-Roses there was no fortunate omen. It represented no common memories, but rather their separate lives and histories, except, indeed, for one brief and unhappy moment which could hardly be called propitious. . . .

Yet it was a really kind and friendly reception which she gave him; and his heart went out to her, when, after *déjeuner*, they talked of quite trivial things, and he sat watching her, her fine hands folded in her lap, in the little faded *salon*, which smelt of flowers. She had always her noble charm, and something of her old beauty, although that was but the pale ghost of what it had once been, and her soft hair, upon which she wore no insincere symbols of widowhood, was but little streaked with gray. She had proposed a stroll in the garden, where a few of its famed roses still lingered, but he made a quick gesture of refusal, and a slight flush, which suffused her pale face, told him that she comprehended his instinctive reluctance.

He fell into a brooding reverie, from which, presently, she softly interrupted him.

'You look remote and sad,' she murmured; 'that is wrong – the sadness! It is a pleasant day, this, for me, and I had hoped it would be the same for you too.'

'I was thinking, thinking,' he said, – 'that I have always missed my happiness.'

Then abruptly, before she could interrupt him, rising and standing before her, his head a little bowed:

'It is late in the day, but, Angèle, will you marry me?'

She was silent for a few minutes, gazing steadily with her calm and melancholy gaze into his eyes, which presently avoided it. Then she said:

'I was afraid that some such notion was in your mind. Yet I am not sorry you have spoken, for it gives me an opportunity, – an occasion of being quite sincere with you, of reasoning.'

'Oh, I am very reasonable,' he said, sadly.

'Yes,' she threw back, quickly. 'And that is why I can speak. No,' she went on, after a moment, 'there is no need to reason with you. My dear old friend, you see yourself as clearly as I do, – examine your heart honestly – you had no real faith in your project, you knew that it was impossible.'

He made no attempt to contradict her.

'You may be right,' he said; 'yes, very likely, you are right. There is a season for all things, for one's happiness as for the rest, and missing it once, one misses it forever. . . . But if things had been different. Oh, Angèle, I have loved you very well!'

She rose in her turn, made a step towards him, and there were tears in her eyes.

'My good and kind old friend! Believe me, I know it, I have always known it. How much it has helped me – through what dark and difficult days – I can say that now: the knowledge of how you felt, how loyal and staunch you were. You were never far away, even in India; and only once it hurt me.' She broke off abruptly, as with a sudden transition of thought; she caught hold of both his hands, and, unresistingly, he followed her into the garden. 'I will not have you take away any bitter memories of this place,' she said with a smile. 'Here, where you once made a great mistake, I should like to have a recantation from your own lips, to hear that you are glad, grateful, to have escaped a great madness, a certain misery.'

'There are some miseries which are like happiness.'

'There are some renunciations which are better than happiness.'

After a while he resumed, reluctantly:

'You are different to other women, you always knew best the needs of your own life. I see now that you would have been miserable.'

'And you?' she asked, quickly.

'I may think your ideal of conduct too high, too hard for poor human flesh. I dare not say you are wrong. . . . But, no, to have known always that I had been the cause of your failing in that ideal, of lowering yourself in your own eyes – that would not have been happiness.'

'That was what I wanted,' she said, quickly.

Later, as he was leaving her – and there had been only vague talk of any further meeting – he said, suddenly:

'I hate to think of your days here; they stretch out with a sort of grayness. How will you live?'

'You forget I have my child, Ursule,' she said. 'She must necessarily occupy me very much now that she is leaving the convent. And you – you have –'

'I have given up my profession.'

'Yes, so much I knew. But you have inherited an estate, have you not?'

'My uncle's place. Yes, I have Beauchamp. I suppose I shall live there. I believe it has been very much neglected.'

'Yes that is right. There is always something to do. I shall like to think of you as a model landlord.'

'Think of me rather as a model friend,' he said, bowing to kiss her hand as he said good-bye to her.

Paris – Pont-Aven, 1896

THE DYING OF FRANCIS DONNE

THE DYING OF FRANCIS DONNE

A STUDY

'Memento homo, quia pulvis es et in pulverem reverteris'

I

He had lived so long in the meditation of death, visited it so often in others, studied it with such persistency, with a sentiment in which horror and fascination mingled; but it had always been, as it were, an objective, alien fact, remote from himself and his own life. So that it was in a sudden flash, quite too stupefying to admit in the first instance of terror, that knowledge of his mortality dawned on him. There was absurdity in the idea too.

'I, Francis Donne, thirty-five and some months old, am going to die,' he said to himself; and fantastically he looked at his image in the glass, and sought, but quite vainly, to find some change in it which should account for this incongruity, just as, searching in his analytical habit into the recesses of his own mind, he could find no such altera-tion of his inner consciousness as would explain or justify his plain conviction. And quickly, with reason and casuistry, he sought to rebut that conviction.

The quickness of his mind – it had never seemed to him so nimble, so exquisite a mechanism of syllogism and deduction – was contraposed against his blind instinct of the would-be self-deceiver, in a conflict to which the latter brought something of desperation, the fierce, agonized desperation of a hunted animal at bay. But piece by piece the chain of evidence was strengthened. That subtile and agile mind of his, with its special knowledge, cut clean through the shrinking protests of instinct, removing them as surely and as remorselessly, he reflected in the image most natural to him, as the keen blade of his surgical knives had removed malignant ulcers.

'I, Francis Donne, am going to die,' he repeated, and, presently, '*I am going to die soon*; in a few months, in six perhaps, certainly in a year.'

Once more, curiously, but this time with a sense of neutrality, as he had often diagnosed a patient, he turned to the mirror. Was it his fancy, or, perhaps, only for the vague light that he seemed to discover a strange gray tone shout his face?

But he had always been a man of a very sallow complexion.

There were a great many little lines, like pen-scratches, scarring the parchment-like skin beneath the keen eyes: doubtless, of late, these had multiplied, become more noticeable, even when his face was in repose.

But, of late, what with his growing practice, his lectures, his writing; all the unceasing labour, which his ambitions entailed, might well have aged him somewhat. That dull, immutable pain, which had first directed his attention from his studies, his investigations, his profession, to his corporal self, the actual Francis Donne, that pain which he would so gladly have called inexplicable, but could explain so precisely, had ceased for the moment. Nerves, fancies! How long it was since he had taken any rest! He had often intended to give himself a holiday, but something had always intervened. But he would do so now, yes, almost immediately; a long, long holiday – he would grudge nothing – somewhere quite out of the way, somewhere, where there was fishing; in Wales, or perhaps in Brittany; that would surely set him right.

And even while he promised himself this necessary relaxation in the immediate future, as he started on his afternoon round, in the background of his mind there lurked the knowledge of its futility; rest, relaxation, all that, at this date, was, as it were, some tardy sacrifice, almost hypocritical, which he offered to powers who might not he propitiated.

Once in his neat brougham, the dull pain began again; but by an effort of will he put it away from him. In the brief interval from house to house – he had some dozen visits to make – he occupied himself with a medical paper, glanced at the notes of a lecture he was giving that evening at a certain Institute on the 'Limitations of Medicine.'

He was late, very late for dinner, and his man, Bromgrove, greeted him with a certain reproachfulness, in which he traced, or seemed to trace, a half-patronizing sense of pity. He reminded himself that on more than one occasion, of late, Bromgrove's manner had perplexed him. He was glad to rebuke the man irritably on some pretext, to dismiss him from the room, and he hurried, without appetite, through the cold or overdone food which was the reward of his tardiness.

His lecture over, he drove out to South Kensington, to attend a reception at the house of a great man – great not only in the scientific world, but also in the world of letters. There was some of the excitement of success in his eyes as he made his way, with smiles and bows, in acknowledgment of many compliments, through the crowded rooms. For Francis Donne's lectures – those of them which were not entirely for the initiated – had grown into the importance of a social function. They had almost succeeded in making science fashionable, clothing its dry bones in a garment of so elegantly literary a pattern. But even in the ranks of the profession it was only the envious, the unsuccessful, who ventured to say that Donne had sacrificed doctrine to popularity, that his science was, in their contemptuous parlance, 'mere literature.'

Yes, he had been very successful, as the world counts success, and his consciousness of this fact, and the influence of the lights, the crowd, the voices, was like absinthe on his tired spirit. He had forgotten, or thought he had forgotten, the phantom of the last few days, the phantom which was surely waiting for him at home.

But he was reminded by a certain piece of news which late in the evening fluttered the now diminished assembly: the quite sudden death of an eminent surgeon, expected there that night, an acquaintance of his own, and more or less of each one of the little, intimate group which tarried to discuss it. With sympathy, with a certain awe, they spoke of him, Donne and others; and both the awe and the sympathy were genuine.

But as he drove home, leaning back in his carriage, in a discouragement, in a lethargy, which was only partly due to physical reaction, he saw visibly underneath their regret – theirs and his own – the triumphant assertion of life, the egoism of instinct. They were sorry, but oh, they were glad! royally glad, that it was another, and not they themselves whom something mysterious had of a sudden snatched away from his busy career, his interests, perhaps from all intelligence; at least, from all the pleasant sensuousness of life, the joy of the visible world, into darkness. And he knew the sentiment, and honestly dared not blame it. How many times had not he, Francis Donne himself experienced it, that egoistic assertion of life in the presence of the dead – the poor, irremediable dead? . . . And now, he was only good to give it to others.

Latterly, he had been in the habit of subduing sleeplessness with injections of morphia, indeed in infinitesimal quantities. But to-night, although he was more than usually restless and awake, by a strong effort of reasonableness he resisted his impulse to take out the little syringe. The pain was at him again with the same dull and stupid insistence; in its monotony, losing some of the nature of pain and becoming a mere nervous irritation. But he was aware that it would not continue like that. Daily, almost hourly, it would gather strength and cruelty; the moments of respite from it would become rarer, would cease. From a dull pain it would become an acute pain, and then a torture, and then an agony, and then a madness. And in those last days, what peace might be his would be the peace of morphia, so that it was essential that, for the moment, he should not abuse the drug.

And as he knew that sleep was far away from him, he propped himself up with two pillows, and by the light of a strong reading lamp settled himself to read. He had selected the work of a distinguished German *savant* upon the cardial functions, and a short treatise of his own, which was covered with recent annotations, in his crabbed handwriting, upon 'Aneurism of the Heart.' He read avidly, and against his own deductions, once more his instinct raised a vain protest. At last he threw the volumes aside, and lay with his eyes shut, without, however, extinguishing the light. A terrible sense of helplessness overwhelmed him; he was seized with an immense and heart-breaking pity for poor humanity as personified in himself; and, for the first time since he had ceased to be a child, he shed puerile tears.

II

The faces of his acquaintance, the faces of the students at his lectures, the faces of Francis Donne's colleagues at the hospital, were altered; were, at least, sensibly altered to his morbid self-consciousness. In every one whom he encountered, he detected, or fancied that he detected, an attitude of evasion, a hypocritical air of ignoring a fact that was obvious and unpleasant. Was it so obvious, then, the hidden horror which he carried incessantly about him? Was his secret, which he would still guard so jealously, become a byword and an anecdote in his little world? And a great rage consumed him against the inexorable and inscrutable forces which had made him to destroy him; against himself, because of his proper impotence; and, above all, against the living, the millions who would remain when he was no longer, the living, of whom many would regret him (some of them his personality, and more, his skill), because he could see under all the unconscious hypocrisy of their sorrow, the exultant self-satisfaction of their survival.

And with his burning sense of helplessness, of a certain bitter injustice in things, a sense of shame mingled; all the merely physical dishonour of death shaping itself to his sick and morbid fancy into a violent symbol of what was, as it were, an actual *moral* or intellectual dishonour. Was not death, too, inevitable and natural an operation as it was, essentially a process to undergo apart and hide jealously, as much as other natural and ignoble processes of the body?

And the animal, who steals away to an uttermost place in the forest, who gives up his breath in a solitude and hides his dying like a shameful thing, – might he not offer an example that it would be well for the dignity of poor humanity to follow?

Since Death is coming to me, said Francis Donne to himself, let me meet it, a stranger in a strange land, with only strange faces round me and the kind indifference of strangers, instead of the intolerable pity of friends.

III

On the bleak and wave-tormented coast of Finistère, somewhere between Quiberon and Fouesnant, he reminded himself of a little fishing-village: a few scattered houses (one of them being an *auberge* at which ten years ago he had spent a night), collected round a poor little gray church. Thither Francis Donne went, without leave-takings or explanation, almost secretly, giving but the vaguest indications of the length or direction of his absence. And there for many days he dwelt, in the cottage which he had hired, with one old Breton woman for his sole attendant, in a state of mind which, after all the years of energy, of ambitious labour, was almost peace.

Bleak and gray it had been, when he had visited it of old, in the late autumn; but now the character, the whole colour of the country was changed. It was brilliant with the promise of summer, and the blue Atlantic, which in winter churned with its long crested waves so boisterously below the little white light-house, which warned mariners (alas! so vainly), against the shark-like cruelty of the rocks, now danced and glittered in the sunshine, rippled with feline caresses round the hulls of the fishing-boats whose brown sails floated so idly in the faint air.

Above the village, on a grassy slope, whose green was almost lurid, Francis Donne lay, for many silent hours, looking out at the placid sea, which could yet be so ferocious, at the low violet line of the Island of Groix, which alone interrupted the monotony of sky and ocean.

He had brought many books with him but he read in them rarely; and when physical pain gave him a respite for thought, he thought almost of nothing. His thought was for a long time a lethargy and a blank.

Now and again he spoke with some of the inhabitants. They were a poor and hardy, but a kindly race: fishers and the wives of fishers, whose children would grow up and become fishermen and the wives of fishermen in their turn. Most of them had wrestled with death; it was always so near to them that hardly one of them feared it; they were fatalists, with the grim and resigned fatalism of the poor, of the poor who live with the treachery of the sea.

Francis Donne visited the little cemetery, and counted the innumerable crosses which testified to the havoc which the sea had wrought. Some of the graves were nameless; holding the bodies of strange seamen which the waves had tossed ashore.

'And in a little time I shall lie here,' he said to himself; 'and here as well as elsewhere,' he added with a shrug, assuming, and, for once, almost sincerely, the stoicism of his surroundings, 'and as lief to-day as to-morrow.'

On the whole, the days were placid; there were even moments when, as though he had actually drunk in renewed vigour from that salt sea air, the creative force of the sun, he was tempted to doubt his grievous knowledge, to make fresh plans for life. But these were fleeting moments, and the reaction from them was terrible. Each day his hold on life was visibly more slender, and the people of the village saw, and with a rough sympathy, which did not offend him, allowed him to perceive that they saw, the rapid growth and the inevitableness of his end.

IV

But if the days were not without their pleasantness, the nights were always horrible – a torture of the body and an agony of the spirit. Sleep was far away, and the brain, which had been lulled till the evening, would awake, would grow electric with life and take strange and abominable flights into the darkness of the pit, into the black night of the unknowable and the unknown.

And interminably, during those nights which seemed eternity, Francis Donne questioned and examined into the nature of that Thing, which stood, a hooded figure beside his bed, with a menacing hand raised to beckon him so peremptorily from all that lay within his consciousness.

He had been all his life absorbed in science; he had dissected, how many bodies? and in what anatomy had he ever found a soul? Yet if his avocations, his absorbing interest in physical phenomena had made him somewhat a materialist, it had been almost without his consciousness. The sensible, visible world of matter had loomed so large to him, that merely to know that had seemed to him sufficient. All that might conceivably lie outside it, he had, without negation, been content to regard as outside his province.

And now, in his weakness, in the imminence of approaching dissolution, his purely physical knowledge seemed but a vain possession, and he turned with a passionate interest to what had been said and believed from time immemorial by those who had concentrated their intelligence on that strange essence, which might after all be the essence of one's personality, which might be that sublimated consciousness – the Soul – actually surviving the infamy of the grave?

> Animula, vagula, blandula!
> Hospes comesque corporis,
> Quae nunc abibis in loca?
> Pallidula, rigida, nudula.

Ah, the question! It was an harmony, perhaps (as, who had maintained? whom the Platonic Socrates in the "Phaedo" had not too successfully refuted), an harmony of life, which was dissolved when life was over? Or, perhaps, as how many metaphysicians had held both before and after a sudden great hope, perhaps too generous to be true, had changed and illuminated, to countless millions, the inexorable figure of Death – a principle, indeed, immortal, which came and went, passing through many corporal conditions until it was ultimately resolved into the great mind, pervading all things? Perhaps? . . . But what scanty consolation, in all such theories, to the poor body, racked with pain and craving peace, to the tortured spirit of self-consciousness so achingly anxious not to be lost.

And he turned from these speculations to what was, after all, a possibility like the others; the faith of the simple, of these fishers with whom he lived, which was also the faith of his own childhood, which, indeed, he had never repudiated, whose practices he had simply discarded, as one discards puerile garments when one comes to man's estate. And he remembered, with the vividness with which, in moments of great anguish, one remembers things long ago familiar, forgotten though they may have been for years, the triumphant declarations of the Church:

> '*Omnes quidem resurgemus, sed non omnes immutabimur. In momento, in ictu oculi, in novissima tuba: canet enim tuba: et mortui resurgent incorrupti, et nos immutabimur. Oportet enim corruptibile hoc induere immortalitatem. Cum autem mortale hoc induerit immortalitatem tunc fiet sermo qui scriptus est: Absorpta est mors in victoria. Ubi est, mors, victoria tua? Ubi est, mors, stimulus tuus?*'

Ah, for the certitude of that! of that victorious confutation of the apparent destruction of sense and spirit in a common ruin. . . . But it was a possibility like the rest; and had it not more need than the rest to be more than a possibility, if it would be a consolation, in that it promised more? And he gave it up, turning his face to the wall, lay very still, imagining himself already stark and cold, his eyes closed, his jaw closely tied (lest the ignoble changes which had come to him should be too ignoble), while he waited until the narrow boards, within which he should lie, had been nailed together, and the bearers were ready to convey him into the corruption which was to be his part.

And as the window-pane grew light with morning, he sank into a drugged, unrestful sleep, from which he would awake some hours later with eyes more sunken and more haggard cheeks. And that was the pattern of many nights.

V

One day he seemed to wake from a night longer and more troubled than usual, a night which had, perhaps, been many nights and days, perhaps even weeks; a night of an ever-increasing agony, in which he was only dimly conscious at rare intervals of what was happening, or of the figures coming and going around his bed: the doctor from a neighbouring town, who had stayed by him unceasingly, easing his paroxysms with the little merciful syringe; the soft, practised hands of a sister of charity about his pillow; even the face of Bromgrove, for whom doubtless he had sent, when he had foreseen the utter helplessness which was at hand.

He opened his eyes, and seemed to discern a few blurred figures against the darkness of the closed shutters through which one broad ray filtered in; but he could not distinguish their faces, and he closed his eyes once more. An immense and ineffable tiredness had come over him, but the pain – oh, miracle! had ceased. . . . And it suddenly flashed over him that this – *this* was Death; this was the thing against which he had cried and revolted; the horror from which he would have escaped; this utter luxury of physical exhaustion, this calm, this release.

The corporal capacity of smiling had passed from him, but he would fain have smiled.

And for a few minutes of singular mental lucidity, all his life flashed before him in a new relief; his childhood, his adolescence, the people whom he had known; his mother, who had died when he was a boy, of a malady from which, perhaps, a few years later, his skill had saved her; the friend of his youth who had shot himself for so little reason; the girl whom he had loved, but who had not loved him. . . . All that was distorted in life was adjusted and justified in the light of his sudden knowledge. *Beati mortui* . . . and then the great tiredness swept over him once more, and a fainter consciousness, in which he could yet just dimly hear, as in a dream, the sound of Latin prayers, and feel the application of the oils upon all the issues and approaches of his wearied sense; then utter unconsciousness, while pulse and heart gradually grew fainter until both ceased. And that was all.

NOTES

Each of Dowson's stories made its original appearance in one of the magazines of the period, the first in *Temple Bar* in January 1888, the last in the *Savoy* in August 1896. The first five were collected in *Dilemmas* in 1895, but the last four were never collected in Dowson's lifetime. Since Dowson oversaw the text of *Dilemmas*, we have followed that text for the first five stories, and the magazine text for the last four, which he had the opportunity to see and usually carefully proof read.

The early negotiations for the publication were with the partnership of Elkin Mathews and John Lane (see page xi above). When the pair split in 1894, Dowson would perhaps have preferred to stay with Lane, whom he knew personally, and two letters to Lane in 1894 (dated August-September in *Letters*, 308) suggest he is trying to meet Lane to discuss the project. By 15 November 1894, however, he is writing to Arthur Symons to tell him that 'I am just going off to visit Elkin Mathews. I am wavering between "Blind Alleys" and "Sentimental Dilemmas" as a title for my stories' (309).

The first edition of *Dilemmas* was published by Elkin Mathews in London and Frederick A. Stokes Company in New York; it was printed by J. Miller and Son, Edinburgh. A draft contract, drawn up by Herbert Horne, to whom Dowson turned for this sort of advice, survives (*Letters*, 437). Mathews agreed to the terms, which stipulated the publishing of six hundred copies of five of Dowson's stories, to be sold at three shillings and sixpence a copy, of which Dowson was to receive sixpence. (This is a fairly inexpensive book – *The Savoy* number 2 cost two shillings and sixpence, and advertised Symons's *London Nights* for six shillings, and two books of poems by Theodore Wratislaw at five shillings each.) The royalty on any American edition was to be threepence a copy. There would be an advance of seven pounds ten shillings, payable on the day of publication. Mathews wished to publish towards the end of November 1894, and advertised the book as in preparation, but it was not in the event published until June 1895.

The second printing of *Dilemmas* (1912) adds nothing: it is a simple reprint of the 1895 text, omitting the notice of a volume of poems in preparation which faced the title page, and omitting the acknowledgement of previous printing from page [vii]. It was published by Elkin Mathews and printed by W. H. Dargan, Ltd., in Smithfield, E. C. The loss of some pieces of type from the corners of pages (the 't' of 'think' on p.103 of that text, the 'd' of 'daily' on p.130) indicates that it was set up from standing type.

We know of only one manuscript for a Dowson story, that for 'A Case of Conscience'. It is manuscript MA 1905 in the Pierpont Morgan Collection in New York. When annotating 'The Eyes of Pride' in his 1947 edition of the stories, Mark Longaker noted that 'There is a MS version of fifteen large foolscap pages at present in the Argus Book Shop, 3 West 46th Street, New York, in which many corrections in Dowson's hand appear' (157). The manuscript of 'A Case of Conscience' now in the Pierpont Morgan Collection conforms to that description except in its title. It is fifteen foolscap pages long ('The Eyes of Pride' is a slightly longer story), is in Dowson's hand, and contains a few corrections. The manuscript was purchased by the library for $56 on 1 March 1958, from a Mrs. Joan Stott, through John Carter, the bibliophile who worked as a consultant to the Morgan Library. We wonder whether Longaker, who does not appear to have seen the manuscript he refers to, may have been in fact describing the manuscript of 'A Case of Conscience' (but see 157 below).

The Diary of a Successful Man

This story was first published in *Macmillan's Magazine,* vol. LXI, in February 1890, 274-281. It is confusingly signed with the initials 'N. B.' although the contents list for the bound volume clearly identifies it as by Ernest Dowson. Dowson was just as confused, and wrote to Charles Sayle on 28th January 1890 that 'My "Diary of a Successful Man" is in "Macmillans" Mag for Feb – although unfortunately – I suppose through a printers error – it has the unaccountable signature of "N. B." I have written to Mowbray Morris to remonstrate. I think the least he can do is to make some form of apology. But editors are a shameless race' (*New Letters from Ernest Dowson,* 17-18).

Dowson reports having 'just finished another *nouvelle,* very short which I want to show you', in a letter to Plarr of c.7 May 1889 (*Letters,* 76); this is probably the 'Diary'. It was accepted in June by Mowbray Morris, editor of *Macmillan's,* which Dowson found 'extremely pink', presumably because it brought in some always-needed cash – Dowson hoped it would earn him at least ten pounds – some of which he planned to spend on a plaque with an idealized likeness of Minnie Terry, his favourite child actress (*Letters,* 132). Dowson reports in a letter of 19 September 1890 that Johnson sent a copy of the story to Pater.

Le Gallienne thought it 'the most original' of the stories, which perhaps explains its place at the beginning of the book.

In revising the text for *Dilemmas,* Dowson changed little, merely indulging in the expectable tinkerings of a writer getting his own work ready for republication. There are a number of, but no significant, changes in punctuation. There are some phrases or words added from time to time: '*revenants*' is added on page 3; '*d'ennui*' and 'To-day' are added on page 4. On page 5, a sentence is added: 'For they married, they must have married, they were made for each other and they knew it'. The fireplace on page 6 becomes 'huge'. At the beginning of the section from the 10th of October, 'to-day' is again added. Dowson adds 'intention of' to the expiation on page 16. There are several changes of words. Dowson replaces 'strongly' with 'potently' on page 3; 'I sometimes fear' with 'I sometimes feel' (4); 'quays' with 'Quais' (4); 'countess' with 'Comtesse' (5); 'bare glimpse' with 'mere glimpse' (5); 'twenty years has' with 'twenty years have' (5); 'more ragged' with 'raggeder' (5); 'subtle' with 'subtile' (6); 'seemed' with 'seems' (8); 'maybe' with 'likely enough' (8); 'by the evening' with 'before the evening' (9); 'wondered' with 'wonder' (10); 'the buried women' with 'those buried women' (10); 'circumstances' with 'circumstance' (12); 'yet hastily' with 'and hastily' (15); 'impostor' with 'fraud' (15). Dowson rewrites the sentence following Delphine's letter, replacing 'It may have been an hour later that I sought out Lorimer with my letter' (9). He is more informed (perhaps he had been discussing it with Lionel Johnson) in his description of the priest: replacing 'the officiating priest in his chasuble and biretta passed from the sacristy and bowed to the altar' with 'the officiating priest in his dalmatic of cloth of gold passed from the sacristy and genuflected at the altar' (14), and replacing 'the one red light that had burnt through the years' with 'the one red light perpetually vigilant' (15).

The Litany of Loretto has the customary prayer and response form. It is the familiar litany of the Blessed Virgin Mary. The first passage quoted invokes Mary: 'Gateway to the heavens, / Morning star, / Health of the sick, Pray for us!' The second passage sees her as: 'Refuge of sinners, / Comforter of the afflicted, / Help of Christians, Pray for us!' The priest's last line is 'Pray for us, O Holy mother of God' to which the voices in the gallery answer 'That we may be made worthy of the promises of Christ.'

Lionel Johnson's poem 'A Descant upon the Litany of Loretto' was not published until *Ireland with Other Poems* (1897, 22-4), but this was a revision of a poem of 1887, and Dowson may have known the earlier version.

A Case of Conscience

Dowson was writing this story in October 1890. He first sent it elsewhere, but when Horne offered to publish something of his, Dowson replied in a letter of ?7 November 1890: 'Your suggestion is most kind & I thank you for it. The story is away at present, but when it returns, as it very probably will, I shall be delighted to give you the next refusal of it. I am a little afraid however that even should it otherwise commend itself to you, you may find its length sufficient ground for rejection: anyhow I will send it to you next' (*Letters*, 175-6). It did prove suitable and was first published in *The Century Guild Hobby Horse*, January, 1891, 2-13. There the text is very heavily punctuated, more so than in the manuscript and more so than in the *Dilemmas* text. The *CGHH* text is larded with commas, it puts colons where semi-colons had been, and the exclamation mark is heavily used. The pointing speaks of an editor (presumably Horne himself) with a love of the antique in language and punctuation, which matches the classicising tone of the magazine. When the text was reprinted in *Dilemmas*, Dowson brought it back nearer to the simpler punctuation of his manuscript.

A manuscript of this story, on fifteen sheets of foolscap, is in the Pierpont Morgan Library, in New York (ms MA 1905). It has all the appearance of being a fair copy rather than a working draft. A small number of words are changed as the transcription proceeds: 'pleasan' is deleted before the word 'good' is substituted to describe the old Bréton servant's face (Dowson usually spelt Bréton with the accent); 'an elastic nature' is substituted for 'a plastic character' to describe the girl (26); 'the setting of his mouth grew a little more rigid' becomes 'the lines about his mouth grew a little sterner' (27); instead of the sun 'lingering', Dowson corrected it to 'dying hard' (27). The fact that the final page has the comment 'Proofs to Ernest Dowson Esq' with his Bridge Dock address and the careful spelling out of '*Ite missa est*' in the margin indicate that this is a fair copy ready for the printer, or just possibly for a typist. (We know of other stories being typed. In a letter of 22 April 1891, he writes of sending 'The Story of a Violin' 'to be typed to the Misses Duff; and so to the various editors'; *Letters*, 193)

The manuscript offers no significant alternative readings, although there are a couple of dozen occasions where it is evident that words have been changed between the manuscript and the printed versions, probably in proof. For the sake of completeness and to indicate how little Dowson changed when he had finished a piece, it seems worth listing the changes (the page reference given is to our text above).

Dilemmas	**Manuscript**
painter (19)	artist
occasionally (19)	absently
built large to an uniform English pattern (20)	built largely; to a stereotyped English pattern
carriage (20)	bearing
vocation (20)	calling
uttering heresy. (20)	uttering heresy, with a kiss.
private (22)	silent
house; an admirable figure, with (22)	house, looking charming with
After a while (22)	Presently
appreciating (23)	digesting
desperately (24)	grimly
the Saint, resenting the purely aesthetic motive of the feat, had seemed to intervene. For (24)	the Saint had presumably resented the artistic purely aesthetic motive of the feat. For
no less (24)	to boot
alone (24)	only
position (25)	opposition (also the *CGHH* reading)
at last (26)	slowly
marry you and find out (27)	marries you and finds out
Angelus bell (27)	Angelus bell, hard by
as it had been very remote (29)	as if it was very remote
intensity (29)	intentness
brush (29)	dressing case
his luggage (29)	their luggage
down the road (30)	up the road
who advanced (30)	which advanced

An Orchestral Violin

First published in the August 1891 issue of *Macmillan's Magazine*, vol. LXIV, 305-314, under the title 'The Story of a Violin'. Le Gallienne did not like the title and when it came time to republish it, Dowson reverted to one he had used earlier.

He first mentions it on 9 November 1889, when he tells Arthur Moore that while waiting for the return of a chapter of their current novel *Felix Martyr*, 'In the meantime I work on a little study of the over critical man and an amourette' (*Letters*, 115). He writes again to Moore on 8 June 1890 that 'I hope to have my story, now in hand, finished early this week – I am going to call it "Fin de Siècle". Parts of it satisfy me more than most things I have done; parts I am afraid are exuberantly bad. It is simply a study of the incomplete amourette of a modern whose critical sense has rather outworn his powers of action – told in the autobiographical manner of both my printed stories. There is more psychological motive in it and less of "ficelle" which Bouthors objected to so in the "Diary"'(*Letters*, 152).

The composition dragged on from 1889 until 1891. On 26 October 1890 he writes of trying 'to finish that interminable story' (*Letters*, 174); by December he has 'nearly finished another *Nouvelle*' (*Letters*, 178); in 22 April 1891, he determines that 'To-night I really intend to finish my present story' (*Letters*, 193); but still in a letter of 10 May 1891 he complains to Moore that 'I can't finish my story; it wants a matter of 10 lines only, this 20 days: but alas! the right ones elude me' (*Letters*, 197). He must have completed it soon afterwards, since he sends a postcard to Moore on 9 June 1891 to say that 'I have finished a story, called "An Orchestral Violin": which the Miss Duffs have typed, & which goes immediately to Mowbray Morris' (*Letters*, 202). On 30 July he could report its publication: 'I have a story, but not at all a satisfactory one in the current "Macmillan"' (*Letters*, 210).

The story in *Dilemmas* has some changes from the *Macmillan's* version. The punctuation is tinkered with: a sprinkling of commas in or out. The spelling is returned to Dowson's preferred traditional and

European versions; 'subtile' for 'subtle', 'enchauntress' for 'enchantress', 'raccounting' for 'recounting'. There are a few verbal alterations: 'replete' (38) replaces 'charged', 'merciless' (42) replaces 'pitiless'; 'no less' (46) replaces 'too'; 'Provençal' (46) replaces 'foreigner'; 'She shot back' (47) replaces 'she cried'; and 'I pondered it, to partake of this quality to be rich' replaces 'I pondered it, to belong to this category, to be rich'. But the significant changes are the addition of a few details which fill out the picture of M. Cristich and slightly more substantial sections to articulate the story. Dowson seems keen to get his picture of Cristich right. The parenthetical detail on page 34 which elaborates Cristich's shabby gentility ' – for his coat was sadly inefficient, and the nap of his carefully brushed hat did not indicate prosperity – ' is new, as is the description of the dress coat 'which seemed to skimp him' on page 38; and Cristich's information about the fine for lateness is slightly amended: 'they fine me, – two shillings and sixpence! that is a good deal, you know, monsieur' becomes 'they fine me two shillings and sixpence, and that I can ill afford, you know, Monsieur' (35). But more interesting are the additions which expand on the mechanics of the story, as if Dowson wishes to indicate what he is doing. The whole of the last paragraph of section II from 'And in effect . . .' (43-44) was added, as if to emphasise the 'ambiguous and unexplained' nature of stories as Dowson conceived them. Also pointing to Dowson's interest in the narrator's role is the addition on page 45, from 'I remember the occasion well' to 'again concerned me'.

Souvenirs of an Egoist

The story was the first of Dowson's stories to be published and appeared in *Temple Bar*, vol 82, 83-98 in January 1888, signed 'Ernest C. Dowson'. It became the fourth story of *Dilemmas*.

Although several years elapsed before it was reprinted, Dowson made few corrections to the text. There are some punctuation changes, which would be tedious to enumerate and uninformative, but the verbal changes are as follows (the page reference is to the present edition):

Dilemmas	*Temple Bar*
I am ignorant whether (54)	I do not suppose
I know that I hated (54)	anyhow, I hated
There it is! (56)	La voilà!
true enough (56)	true enough, anyhow.
on the quai. (57	by the Madeleine.
we might move. (57)	we might go now.
The *ménage* of Ninette was a strange one! (57)	Poor Ninette, her *ménage* was a strange one.
not precisely a pretty child, (58)	not a pretty child exactly,
face was very attractive, (58)	face became very taking,
showed (61)	shewed
Felix, whose principles are adapted to his conscience and whose conscience is bounded by the law, (62)	Felix, who carries as light a load of principles as it is possible for a man to do with and escape the clutch of the law,
a charming composition (64)	a charming water-colour
and that was true. (64)	which was true.
seized me, (65)	seized on me,
such strange music (65)	such music
two or three finer (66)	scores of finer
here in England. (66)	here in London.
Shade of Musset, who is (66)	Who is
Soeurs de la Miséricorde (66)	Orphanage
already be hating each other. (67)	be hating each other like poison already.
repugnance towards me. (68)	repugnance for me.
the great Pan, (69)	the great god Pan,
my art: and that you know. (69)	my art.
merely human love. (71)	mere human love.
no awakening, (71)	no awaking,

Eheu Fugaces, with which the story begins, are the first words of Horace's Ode XIV in Book II, where Horace laments the inexorable slipping away of time.

The Statute of Limitations

This story was first printed in *The Hobby Horse* (the new incarnation of *The Century Guild Hobby Horse,* now published by Elkin Mathews), Number 1, MDCCCXCIII, 2-8, which probably came out in late summer, although Dowson wrote to Horne on 5 February 1893 to ask 'How goes the "Hobby" now? I suppose we may soon expect it' (*Letters*, 268). He refers to a story 'recently published in the "Hobby Horse"' in his letter to Mathews in late November 1893 (*Letters*, 301). This became the last story in *Dilemmas*.

Dowson probably began this story in May 1892. In August he was trying to complete it with the intention of sending it to *Macmillan's*, but he was eventually pleased to be able to offer it to *The Hobby Horse*. In sending the story to Herbert Horne, Dowson commented that 'I do not feel at all sure that you will like the story; it is only for very obscure reasons that I do, myself. You shall have the refusal of it however with pleasure. I need not say how charmed I shall be, if you find it worthy to be shrined in the new Hobby' (*Letters*, 252-3). Perhaps the obscure reasons for liking it relate to his friendship with Charles Winstanley Tweedy (1867-1909), a bosom friend in the late eighties, who departed for Chile in 1890 (see *Letters*, 170). Horne obviously took his editorial duties seriously and made many suggestions on Dowson's manuscript. Dowson's reply of 2 December 1892 is of interest in understanding his attitude to his work: 'A great many of your alterations I will adopt; some I should wish to on their intrinsic merits, but fear, that in doing so, I should undeniably destroy the rhythm; a few I do not quite care about' (*Letters*, 256). In February 1893 he thanks Horne for the 'revise', probably of this story.

Horne had not suggested punctuation as lavish as he seems to have done with 'A Case of Conscience', but Dowson made it less heavy when he revised it for *Dilemmas*. He had proofed it well for the *Hobby*, and the only variant other than punctuation is 'chain' for 'chains' (78), possibly a misprint

Apple Blossom in Brittany

This story was first published in *The Yellow Book,* volume III in October 1894, 93-109. Flower and Maas think that this is likely to be the story which Dowson sends in a letter to Arthur Moore of 4 March 1891: 'the MSS of my last story – a typed version of which is now on its way to Mowbray Morris. May he be merciful' (*Letters*, 186). Morris obviously wasn't merciful. They also think that, when Dowson writes to Horne on 31 July 1892 that 'I entirely forgot to return you the enclosed proof', he is referring to 'Apple Blossom in Brittany'.

Dowson had a very specific notion of Ploumariel in spite of its fictionality. It occurs here and in 'A Case of Conscience'. In a letter to Arthur Moore of 1890 or 1891, he writes that 'I want the summer & "Ploumariel", with the advantage of your company' (*Letters*, 146).

The Eyes of Pride

Longaker in 1947 reported a fifteen page manuscript version in the Argus Book Shop in New York, but we have not seen it, and the manuscript in question could possibly be that for 'A Case of Conscience' (see above, 148). There is however a draft of a business letter to an unidentified correspondent (*Letters*, 311) on the back of a page of the manuscript of 'The Eyes of Pride' recorded by Flower and Maas as 'Formerly property of Mr. Ben Abramson', which we have not seen.

The story was first published in the first number of *The Savoy* in January 1896, 51-63.

The dedication is again to Adelaide Foltinowicz, Dowson's 'Missie', to whom he dedicated *Dilemmas*. The quotation is the last two lines of sonnet XXIV of *Modern Love*, Meredith's sequence of fifty 16-line sonnets anatomising the disintegration of a marriage. In sonnet XXIV, the speaker is tempted by the apparent purity of the woman he loves. There are many elements which would attract Dowson to the poem:

> The misery is greater, as I live!
> To know her flesh so pure, so keen her sense,
> That she does penance now for no offence,
> Save against Love. The less can I forgive!

The less can I forgive, though I adore
That cruel lovely pallor which surrounds
Her footsteps; and the low vibrating sounds
That come on me, as from a magic shore.
Low are they, but most subtle to find out
The shrinking soul. Madam, 'tis understood
When women play upon their womanhood,
It means, a Season gone. And yet I doubt
But I am duped. That nun-like look waylays
My fancy. Oh! I do but wait a sign!
Pluck out the eyes of pride! thy mouth to mine!
Never! though I die thirsting. Go thy ways!

Dowson reported to Edgar Jepson in a letter of November 1895 that 'I have sent off my story to it [*The Savoy*], and am tolerably satisfied with it — in fact it is the best I have done — except perhaps that in the "Yellow Book"' (*Letters*, 319).

Countess Marie of the Angels

This story was first published in the second number of *The Savoy* in April 1896, 173-183, just before the continuation of Beardsley's 'Under the Hill'.

A long letter to Arthur Moore over the Christmas period of 1895 from Paris describes what he is working at and reports that 'I have also promised another story for No 2 of the Savoy but so far have no idea of what it will be about – but I suppose the scene must be in or about Paris' (*Letters*, 336). When he writes of it to Moore, he again stresses the Parisian theme: 'I have just sent off a story I have succeeded in finishing here to that notorious publication [*The Savoy*]. It is supposed to appear in the forthcoming number, but my delay may have rendered that too late. It is called "Countess Marie of the Angels" & the maiden name of its heroine is Marie-Joseph Angèle de la Tour de Boiserie! Good old Faubourg St. Germain!' (*Letters*, 348).

The dedication is to Jean de Tinan (1875-1899), an author with whom Dowson was friendly in Paris in the second half of the nineties. Dowson proposed to write a notice in *The Savoy* to include mention of Tinan's

Erythrée in 1896, but nothing came of it, perhaps because, as he admitted to Davray, he didn't appreciate it. Tinan was involved in the setting up of a French magazine in imitation of *The Savoy*, called *Le Centaure*.

The Dying of Francis Donne

This story - or study as he preferred to call it - was first published in the fourth number of *The Savoy* in August 1896, the same volume as contained Arthur Symons's 'A Literary Causerie: – On a Book of Verses', the essay which acted as the foundation of the 'Dowson myth'.

It was written at Pont-Aven, where Dowson was writing and translating. His response to Leonard Smithers in early April 1896 shows that he is under continuous pressure of work: 'I duly note your require-ments & will do my best to fulfil them. The story is already under weigh. My studies have been interrupted the last day or two by the Easter festivities – & fair – when this town is en fête it is terribly difficult to work, and the arrival of a Parisian acquaintance [Maurice Cremnitz], with an introduction from Jean de Tinan. / No more for the moment. I will send "Pucelle" tomorrow, I hope, & the proofs [of his pieces for the April *Savoy*: 'Countess Marie of the Angels' and 'Saint-Germain-en-Laye'] by return when they arrive' (*Letters*, 352). Towards the end of April he reassures Smithers that 'My story or study rather will not be too long for one number' (*Letters*, 358).

When Lionel Johnson wrote 'Ash Wednesday; In Memoriam Ernest Dowson' (published in *The Outlook* of 20 January 1900) he used as a refrain the words 'Memento, homo, quia pulvis es', the words used on Ash Wednesday which warn: 'Remember, O man, that you are dust and will return to dust.'

The Latin lines beginning 'Animula, vagula, blandula' are reputed to have been composed by the Emperor Hadrian just before his death (*Hadrianus*, XXV). Dowson probably derived them from that important source for him, Pater's *Marius the Epicurean*, where they form the epigraph to chapter VIII at the beginning of Part the Second, and are annotated: 'The Emperor Hadrian to his Soul'. The lines quoted, whose repeated diminutives it is difficult to catch, can be translated:

> Little soul, uncertain, charming,
> Guest and companion of my body,
> To what place will you now go?
> Pale, inflexible, and naked.

Like Pater, Dowson leaves off the last line, 'nec ut soles dabis iocos' ('and not, as you used to be, full of fun'), which was perhaps too light for his context.

The Latin quotation which he remembers – *'Omnes quidem resurgemus . . .'* – is the Vulgate's version of the First Epistle of Paul to the Corinthians, chapter 15, verses 51ff, which in the Authorised Version reads as follows:

> We shall not all sleep, but we shall all be changed, in a moment, in the twinkling of an eye, at the last trump: for the trumpet shall sound, and the dead shall be raised incorruptible, and we shall be changed. For this corruptible must put on incorruption, and this mortal must put on immortality. So when this corruptible shall have put on incorruption, and this mortal shall have put on immortality, then shall be brought to pass the saying that is written, Death is swallowed up in victory. O death, where is thy sting? O grave, where is thy victory?

FURTHER READING

Dowson's Works (listed chronologically)

A Comedy of Masks (novel, with Arthur Moore), 1893.

La Terre by Emile Zola (translation), 1894.

Majesty by Louis Couperus (translation with A. Teixeira de Mattos), 1894.

Dilemmas: Stories and Studies in Sentiment, 1895 and 1912.

The History of Modern Painting by Richard Muther (translation with George A. Greene and Arthur C. Hillier), 1895-6.

La fille aux yeux d'or by Honoré de Balzac (translation), 1896.

Verses, 1896.

The Pierrot of the Minute, a dramatic phantasy in one act, 1897.

Les liaisons dangeureuses by Choderlos de Laclos (translation), 1898.

Adrian Rome (novel, with Arthur Moore), 1899.

La Pucelle by Voltaire (edition with some original translation), 1899.

Memoirs of Cardinal Dubois by Paul Lacroix (translation), 1899.

Decorations: in Verse and Prose, 1899.

The Poems of Ernest Dowson, ed. Thomas B. Mosher, Portland, Maine, 1902.

The Poems of Ernest Dowson, with a memoir by Arthur Symons, 1905.

Cynara: a Little Book of Verse, Portland, Maine, 1907.

The Confidantes of a King. The Mistresses of Louis XV by Edmond and Jules de Goncourt (translation), 1907.

Poems and Prose, with a memoir by Arthur Symons, New York, 1919.

Complete Poems, New York, 1928.

The Poetical Works of Ernest Dowson, ed. Desmond Flower, 1934, 1950 and 1967.

The Stories of Ernest Dowson, ed. Mark Longaker, 1947.

The Poems of Ernest Dowson, ed. Mark Longaker, Philadelphia, 1962.

The Letters of Ernest Dowson, ed. Desmond Flower and Henry Maas, 1967.

New Letters from Ernest Dowson, ed. Desmond Flower, Andoversford, 1984.

Other Works to Consult

Victor Plarr, *Ernest Dowson 1888-1897: Reminiscences, Unpublished Letters and Marginalia*, 1914.

W. R. Thomas, 'Ernest Dowson at Oxford', *Nineteenth Century*, CIII (April, 1928), 560-566.

Marion Plarr, *Cynara. The Story of Ernest and Adelaide* (fictionalised biography), 1933.

John Gawsworth, 'The Dowson Legend' in *Essay by Divers Hands*, n.s. vol XVII, ed. E. H. W. Meyerstein, 1938; reprinted as *The Dowson Legend*, 1939.

Mark Longaker, *Ernest Dowson*, Philadelphia, 1944, revised 1945 and 1967.

Thomas Burnett Swann, *Ernest Dowson*, New York, 1964.

John R. Reed, 'Bedlamite and Pierrot: Ernest Dowson's Esthetic of Futility', *ELH*, 35 (1968), 94-113.

Jonathan Ramsey, 'Ernest Dowson: An Annotated Bibliography of Writings About Him', *English Literature in Transition*, 14 (1971), 17-42.

Laurence Dakin, *Ernest Dowson, The Swan of Lee*, Montreal, 1972.

Keith Cushman, 'The Quintessence of Dowsonism: "The Dying of Francis Donne"', *Studies in Short Fiction*, 11 (1974), 45-51.

Chris Snodgrass, 'Ernest Dowson's Aesthetics of Contamination', *English Literature in Transition*, 26 (1983), 162-174.

John R. Reed, 'From Aestheticism to Decadence: Evidence from the Short Story', *Victorians Institute Journal*, 11 (1982-3), 1-12; abridged in his *Decadent Style*, Athens, Ohio U. P., 1985.

Ruth Y. Jenkins, 'A Note on Conrad's Sources: Ernest Dowson's "The Statute of Limitations" as Source for *Heart of Darkness*', *English Language Notes*, 24 (March 1987), 39-42.

G. A. Cevasco, *Three Decadent Poets, Ernest Dowson, John Gray, and Lionel Johnson: An Annotated Bibliography*, New York, 1990.

Chris Snodgrass, 'Aesthetic Memory's Cul-de-sac: The Art of Ernest Dowson', *English Literature in Transition*, 35 (1992), 26-53.

R. K. R. Thornton, 'Ernest Dowson', *Dictionary of Literary Biography*, 135, Washington, 1994, 96-105.

Jean-Jacques Chardin, *Ernest Dowson (1867-1900) et la crise fin de siècle anglaise*, Paris, 1995.

Jad Adams, *Madder Music, Stronger Wine: The Life of Ernest Dowson, Poet and Decadent*, 2000.